AN AGREEABLE ARRANGEMENT

Other books by Shirley Marks:

Geek to Chic
Honeymoon Husband
Miss Quinn's Quandary

AN AGREEABLE ARRANGEMENT

•

Shirley Marks

AVALON BOOKS
NEW YORK

Published by Thomas Bouregy & Co., Inc.
160 Madison Avenue, New York, NY 10016

Library of Congress Cataloging-in-Publication Data

Marks, Shirley.
An agreeable arrangement / Shirley Marks.
    p.   cm.
ISBN 978-0-8034-9937-9 (acid-free paper)   1. Inheritance
and succession—Fiction.   2. England—Fiction.   I. Title.
PS3613.A7655A73 2009
813'.6—dc22

2008031622

PRINTED IN THE UNITED STATES OF AMERICA
ON ACID-FREE PAPER
BY HADDON CRAFTSMEN, BLOOMSBURG, PENNSYLVANIA

To Faith for seeing the charm in my stories
and
To Kim for her persistent enthusiasm
to hear every word in every book—
and believing as I do that Faith is awesome!

As always . . . to my darling husband.

A special acknowledgement to
Heidi Ashworth who allowed her
characters Sir Anthony Crenshaw
and Lord Avery from
Miss Delacourt Speaks Her Mind,
an AVALON Historical Romance,
to make a cameo appearance in this book.

Chapter One

"**H**edgeway Park is and always will be my heart's desire," Lady Cassandra Phillips said to no one in particular. "If it is my fate to reside here for all my remaining days, it could not make me happier."

Cassie looked at the house and the manicured gardens that stretched around her home before she climbed the stone steps to the garden terrace. She sat in one of the chairs, shaded by a yew tree. Mrs. Hicks, who had followed from the house, carried a pitcher of lemonade. She offered a glass to Cassie then set the tray on the terrace table.

"Where is the pet?" Mrs. Hicks glanced about for a sign of him. "Romeo? Romeo? Where art thou, Romeo?"

"I do wish you would not call for him in that manner," Cassie scolded her housekeeper.

"You should have given his name a bit more consideration before you presented him with such a burden."

"I'm sure you'll find him in some cozy place for an afternoon nap. His morning began with chasing the rabbits from the vegetable patch. There was a large one that led him on an exhaustive chase."

"The one with a torn ear?" The housekeeper closed her eyes and steeled herself. "Ah, he's a devil that one is, sneaking through the thatched fences, around the makeshift barriers, the staff's clever traps and the like." She mimicked his movements with a sideways, snake-like wave of her arm. "It's impossible to keep him out of the garden. The cook'll sooner add him to her stew or make a nice meat pie, if'n she had the chance."

"Well, he has exhausted Romeo quite completely. I'm certain that my pet will have thoroughly recovered once he smells cook's cakes come out of the oven." Cassie pulled out the chair next to her. "Pray, sit with me, Rosie."

"You know the help shouldn't be taking tea with you, milady."

"Bother, you know I don't consider you a servant. I think of you as family. You nearly raised me yourself after Mama died. And you've been a constant comfort after Papa's death." Cassie gave her a smile. "Besides, this is lemonade, not tea. Now, I beg you, sit."

" 'Tis really not right." Mrs. Hicks hesitated but she finally sat. "You should find a proper lady's companion, not an old servant. What would people think?"

"I don't give a fig what people think," Cassie said with complete sincerity.

"Really, milady, I have the household to run."

"I mean no offense but you are not as young as you once were. You should let Molly take on some responsibilities."

"She is but a child," Mrs. Hicks gasped.

"You only wish to see her as such. I'm sure she could run the house quite competently. I do wish you would agree to become my companion. I still need a bit of guidance now and again."

"What you need is a husband," Mrs. Hicks told her.

Cassie had no reason nor wish to marry. She did not need the protection or financial support of a man. Life was perfect. Her father had seen to that. He'd left her a tidy sum and her home, Hedgeway Park.

"You are far from being an old maid. You still could make a decent match. If you'd only try," Mrs. Hicks implored with the tilt of her head. "I know your father would have wanted you to marry."

"Fustian! Papa had made plans but he wasn't really set on seeing them through. They were an old man's folly, that's all." Cassie made a moue. "Now, look here, Lavette has brought down these magazines. I do wish you would help me look through them."

The housekeeper set her pince-nez on the bridge of her nose to examine the fashion plates.

"Lavette mentioned that some of my gowns need to be replaced. I hate to spend the money but I fear she is right." Cassie handed Mrs. Hicks a few magazines.

"I believe you've always felt that practical clothes were best for a practical woman," Mrs. Hicks stated.

"You know me too well." Cassie began to look for a dress that might appeal to her. "I must admit that I am ready for a change."

The drab apparel she wore was not her favorite by half. Thank goodness today was the last day of mourning. Although no amount of time would ease the pain of her father's absence, she could look forward to wearing the clothes she had cast off two years prior.

A shadow fell across the magazine Cassie read.

"Excuse me, my lady." Siddons the butler neared. "This arrived only moments ago." He lowered the salver. Cassie retrieved the letter. Siddons and his tray retreated into the house.

Cassie recognized the scrawl across the front of the missive. If correct, this should be the list of first quarter expenses from the squire, Julian Stewart, the executor of her father's will.

"That man is so timely, you could set a clock by his letter's arrival," Mrs. Hicks remarked in good humor.

For the last two years, the financial breakdown of the previous quarter had always arrived on the first day of the second month of the subsequent quarter. Cassie broke open the seal and straightened the single, crisp sheet of paper.

Instead of the column of numbers on the right side of the page and their corresponding descriptions on the left, this was a short note.

Cassie's eyes went wide. She felt the blood drain from her face. She sat bolt upright, sending the fashion plates tumbling from her lap onto the ground.

"What is it? What's happened?" Mrs. Hicks sat up in alarm.

Cassie said nothing. The housekeeper took the letter and read the news for herself.

"Oh, my!" was all she could manage at first. "I was afraid your father would do something like this." Mrs. Hicks moaned, echoing Cassie's dread.

"This is simply too much!" Cassie refused to believe this was happening to her. "I cannot go through with this!"

"But dear"—Mrs. Hicks laid a hand upon Cassie's trembling arm—"this says if you do not marry Edward Stewart, you'll lose everything: The money your father put aside for you and Hedgeway Park!"

Cassie spun into her bedroom in a flurry. "Have my trunks brought down and pack my clothes, Lavette. In two days' time, we shall be leaving for Stewart Hall."

Lavette came in from the dressing room. "Most

of zee wardrobe 'ave already finished airing. I 'ave brought in your muslin dresses, zee silk and satin gowns will be finished in plenty of time."

"Not those clothes. I wish to bring only my mourning clothes."

"*Pourquoi*? Today eez the last day you need to wear those dresses. You should arrive in your lovely blue traveling dress. It should make such a stunning entrance. Zat evening, you could appear at dinner in your pink silk." Lavette palmed her hands together and twirled. "And what a sensation you shall make when you attend your first soiree in zee yellow satin gown." The maid needed little help in imagining the romantic notion of attending a ball.

"Lavette, there will be no balls, no soirees, no parties," Cassie answered, her tone serious, her mood somber. "I plan to convince the squire that I am still mourning my father. I hope it will delay or even prevent my marriage to Edward Stewart."

"Prevent zee marriage? Eez not marriage what all English gentlewomen desire?"

"Not *this* gentlewoman." Cassie sat at her dressing table and stared into the pier glass. Part of her knew that she might be forced to marry the younger Stewart brother. But not if she could prevent it. "I shan't marry for convenience or for a silly whim of my father's."

"Must there be a *reason* for you to marry? Ah, *l'amour* . . . then love, perhaps, no?" Lavette's lips bowed into a soft curve.

"I would gladly marry for love," Cassie lamented. "If such a fortunate thing were ever to find me."

In two days time a carriage sent by Squire Stewart had arrived. A pair of matched dappled grays drew the large black closed carriage which stood parked in the drive. Standing outside the front door, Mrs. Hicks sniffed into a handkerchief, muffling her sobs. With the luggage loaded, the transport waited for its the final passenger.

"Don't worry, Rosie," Cassie whispered to the housekeeper. "I have Lavette with me and if all goes well, I shall return within the week." Cassie braved a smile, urging Mrs. Hicks not to despair.

"Romeo!" Cassie called out. The small brown and white terrier came bounding from around the house. He darted toward his mistress and ran a tight circle around her legs. Cassie handed him to Lavette, already seated in the carriage. Cassie boarded and sat upon the burgundy seats that smelled of new leather.

"A safe trip, my lady," Siddons said over the creaking of the springs of the coach.

With a crack of the driver's whip, the horses were off and the carriage started to move.

Cassie waved good-bye. The last glimpse of Hedgeway Park secured her a dismal view of Mrs. Hicks succumbing to another bout of tears.

Every mile away from Hedgeway Park made Cassie question her resistance. Every mile toward

Stewart Hall made her realize how much she loved her home and what she would do to secure its ownership.

After the first few hours, Cassie wanted to order the driver to turn back for Yorkshire, but reined the temptation. Sitting in silence, she planned.

At first, Cassie thought to tell the squire that she was in love with another. However that was far from the truth. Perhaps she could feign illness. That would mean she'd have to be near death now to warrant a recuperation that would take more than several months. Still that would only postpone her fate. She needed a solid reason not to marry Edward Stewart.

Cassie was not comfortable approaching her father's executor with a lie. An honest, straightforward manner might yield the best results. Yes, she decided, that might just work.

After the day's travel, the carriage pulled up to the Dog and Harp Inn for the night. Despite the name, the proprietors of the establishment did not cater to dogs, whether or not accompanied by harps. The innkeeper wanted to put Romeo in the stable with the rest of the livestock. Cassie would not allow such treatment of her pet and carried the terrier off to her room.

Cassie and Lavette entered their accommodations. Romeo trotted around, found himself a warm spot in front of the meagerly lit hearth and curled before it.

"This room eez barely passable, my lady." Lavette lifted the sheets on the bed, inspecting them. "These linens have not been properly aired."

Cassie pulled the maid from the bed. "It is but for one night. This will suffice."

An hour had passed when a knock on the door announced supper. The meal of meat stew, sliced bread and tea remained untouched by Cassie and Lavette. Romeo cleaned every spoonful, leaving the innkeeper to think the guests had truly enjoyed the culinary fare.

"Do put yourself to bed, Lavette. Our travels will end tomorrow. We must get our rest." Lavette turned in for the night. Cassie took her own advice and slipped between the cold sheets after changing into her night rail.

Cassie managed to close out the distant sounds of voices and rowdiness from the tavern below. The fire crackled in the background while Lavette's quiet snores rumbled in counterpoint to those of the terrier. In no time at all, Cassie fell asleep.

The next morning a knock at the door announced the arrival of breakfast. Lavette answered the door. She set the toast-and-muffin-laden tray on the table near the fire, where Cassie sat.

It would be another full day's travel ahead of them. Cassie took the *Gazette* that arrived with the tray. She unfolded the journal and perused the front page.

Hostilities were growing between the Colonies and England. Napoleon's ships still threatened English trading vessels. None of which interested her.

Cassie ignored the increasing flutter she felt. Lavette poured a cup of tea and placed a biscuit on a plate for her mistress. The subsequent growl from Cassie's stomach was not from hunger. It was nerves that plagued her. Her stomach, bound into a tight knot, would not permit her to relax.

Cassie turned the page. Staring at her from the third page she saw an announcement that bore her name. It read:

Julian Stewart announces the engagement of Lady Cassandra Phillips, daughter to the late Earl of Thaddbury, to his brother, Edward Stewart. The ceremony will take place on June 18th.

Cassie gasped. The day before her birthday! How insufferable! And there it was, for all of England to see.

"Of all the inconsiderate, deceitful tricks!" In a crisp motion, Cassie lifted the paper and folded it, displaying the offensive notice on top.

Didn't he know? It was proper for only the bride's family to publish an announcement. But she had no family. Still, that did not give him the authority to do such a thing.

The nerve of the man! Cassie would make him print a retraction right away.

But how, she wondered, would she ever convince him that the marriage would not take place?

Chapter Two

The transport lumbered up the drive of Stewart Hall. Cassie scarcely noticed how much London had grown after ten years. The vehicle came to a halt and the door opened.

She fairly leaped out, brushed past the footman in the black and gold livery that had assisted her, and gave the other footman, heading for the entrance, no opportunity to knock and announce her arrival. She had no difficulty flinging wide the heavy front door of Stewart Hall with the anger and outrage that fueled her strength.

The butler bowed, his composure intact. "May I announce you?"

"I'll announce myself, thank you." Cassie took a

handful of her gray skirt and spun away. With reticule swinging by her side and the *Gazette* clutched in her hand, she continued unescorted down the long hall, looking for a sign of the squire. She tried to conjure the ideas she'd thought of during the journey to persuade him into changing his mind.

From the far doorway, Julian Stewart appeared, tall and lean. He looked vaguely familiar. Of course, he was taller now. He was a young man of fourteen the last time she had seen him. She recognized the same wave in his hair, the same angular lines of his face, and the same dark, unreadable eyes. On the fourth finger of his left hand Cassie noticed the signet ring she had seen his father wear.

At the tender age of nine, she thought herself to be in love with young Julian. He'd shown about as much interest in her then as he did now. None.

Bits of the speech she memorized came back to her but the closer Cassie neared the more difficult she found it to keep her anger restrained.

"How dare you make an engagement announcement on my behalf!" Cassie shook the paper only inches from his nose. Her built-up frustration crossed the line of decorum, her self-control fled and she slapped his face. What she really wanted to do was level her reticule at his head. "I cannot conceive of a more presumptuous . . ."

The increasing noise of the footmen hauling

luggage into the house interrupted Cassie's tirade. Lavette supervised, spouting in French, warning the footmen to take care with the trunks.

The squire backed into his library, escaping the disturbance. "If you wish me to retract the announcement, Lady Cassandra, it is simply out of the question." Touching the reddened area on his cheek, he winced.

"I implore you, sir, do you have any sympathy for your brother?" Cassie thought perhaps if Edward Stewart had also objected to this marriage, that might sway the squire into helping them avoid the parson's mousetrap.

"This arrangement was made long ago." The squire took a seat behind his Sheridan desk.

"That is precisely the point, sir," Cassie continued. "Edward and I were mere children. You cannot expect us to go through with that arrangement after all this time."

"Our fathers fully expected that you both would honor their wishes. As executor of your father's will, the late Earl of Thaddbury, it is my duty to see this marriage take place." The squire lifted his wire-rimmed glasses off the blotter. "I, myself, had such a match made and married younger than you and Edward are now and it worked out splendidly."

"And your wife, sir, what does she have to say?"

The squire guided each ear piece to its resting place with precision. "My wife passed away some years ago." He opened the inkwell and took up his quill.

"My condolences." *Mrs. Stewart probably died of extreme cold due to direct exposure to her husband.*

The squire dipped the quill and began to pen his letter, not looking up from his work. It was clear to Cassie this man expected unconditional obedience from her and would accept no less.

"As for matrimonial affection, no doubt Edward will grow fond of you and you him, in time."

Cassie stood in front of his desk clutching her reticule. She bit the inside of her cheek to keep herself from saying something she would, no doubt, later regret.

"Why now?" she asked.

"There has been more than sufficient time for mourning. Your father clearly stated you should marry Edward before your twentieth birthday." He paused, taking a moment to think on the matter. "Quite frankly, I believe Edward needed the time as well. I don't think he was ready for marriage any sooner than this. It is beyond my imagination that Edward could ever be a settled, happily wedded man."

"Until now." Cassie found it hard to believe that this cold and completely unfeeling man could even consider the wishes of his younger brother.

The squire went on with his discourse. "Although our contact was limited our fathers' were not. They conferred with one another on personal and business matters up until my father's death. The late earl continued to entrust me with their business matters and I expect that your children will be the proper heir that both of them would have wanted. Wealth and land holdings from both sides of the family, and a possible title from your father should your cousin lack issue."

Cassie felt her face warm at his casual mention of such an intimate subject. She dropped her gaze away from him.

The squire took that opportunity to facilitate her exit. "Maxwell will have you shown to your rooms. Edward should make his appearance shortly and you two can reacquaint yourselves."

"There must be something short of marrying Edward that I can do to keep Hedgeway Park? Please, sir, will you not help me?" Cassie began to sound desperate.

Squire Stewart paused, his pen lifted in midsentence. "Kindly curtail your sorrowful pleas, Lady Cassandra. In the end, you shall do as you are instructed." There was no anger in the squire's voice.

"After the wedding you and Edward shall move to your beloved home for the duration if that is what you wish. Until that time, this is where you will reside. Good day to you." He returned to his work papers.

The butler loomed in the doorway and called to Cassie, "This way please, my lady."

How very rude the squire was. Without say in the

matter and without other viable options, Cassie spun away and followed the butler.

Cassie stopped in the foyer. Lavette stood with the luggage and waited for a word from her mistress. "We will be staying, Lavette," Cassie said, unhappy with the outcome of her appeal. She glared over her shoulder, down a long hallway at Julian Stewart who sat at his desk. He seemed unaffected and continued with his work. It was obvious to her that he gave her not another thought.

Maxwell stopped in the foyer. He made the introduction, "Lady Cassandra, the housekeeper, Mrs. Green." Then left.

"Your ladyship." A stout woman stopped in front of Cassie and dipped a curtsy. "This way please, my lady." She lifted the hem of her skirts and mounted the steps.

Cassie took hold of the heavy oak handrail and trudged up the stairs of this unfamiliar house she would not call home.

Mrs. Green stood to the left side of the landing. "Miss Lorna's rooms are across from yours."

A picture of Lorna as a small child flashed in Cassie's mind. Lorna, the only sister of the Stewarts, had been four or five the last time Cassie had seen her.

The housekeeper opened the double doors to Cassie's apartments and stepped into the room.

Rounding the far hallway corner came a young

man—Edward Stewart, younger brother of the squire. He was dressed in buckskin breeches that hugged his well-shaped muscular thighs and disappeared into his black high-top boots. The dark green riding jacket brought out the most vivid green of his eyes, which would make the prettiest girl envious.

His pace quickened and a smile brightened on what Cassie considered a most handsome face. Edward indeed resembled his older brother Julian. Although his coloring was fair and the elder's dark, they stood about the same height.

Edward's face was a bit fuller and had a healthy glow. His head was topped by riotous blond curls. It took only a moment for Cassie to decide Edward was more attractive and far more likeable of the two brothers.

"Can it truly be you? My dear Cass!" Edward took her hand and performed a deep, sweeping bow. He applied a light kiss on the back of her hand before he rose. "Do you not remember me? *Edward.*" A slight tilt of his head off to one side questioned whether or not she recognized him.

Of course she had. If circumstances had been different, she might have been more pleased to remake his acquaintance. In her present situation, she could not bring herself to say she was truly as glad to see him as he was to see her.

"It's been a very long time, I fear. We were what . . . both nine? Mere children then but *how* you have grown." With her hand in his, he took a small step back and eyed her, making a thorough inspection. He smiled. His eyes smiled. "I must say, time has been more than generous to you."

Cassie felt her face warm. She was not accustomed to men staring at her in such an open and obvious fashion.

"After you're settled, please allow me the pleasure of escorting you for a walk around the gardens."

"That sounds wonderful. I shall look forward to it."

Edward led her with the hand he would not relinquish. He slipped his other around her waist and stepped behind her, escorting her to her rooms.

"Until this afternoon, then." Edward pressed his lips against the back of her hand and whispered, "No need to blush for we are to spend the rest of our lives together and I shall not waste precious moments being proper when there is no need."

He reached the top of the stairs and turned to face her. In a bout of dramatics, Edward tossed another kiss from his fingertips before descending.

Cassie could not help but smile at the sweet intent of the romantic gesture. With his exit, Cassie passed across the threshold and studied the bedchamber. She admired the large–paned windows that allowed the bright rays of the sun to cascade into the room. Moving farther in, she ran her fingers over the back of the gilded sofa in front of the fireplace.

Turning to the right, she crossed to the writing table,

strategically placed near the windows where one could pen letters in natural light.

Cassie would need to write Mrs. Hicks and tell her of the bad news. She had no real notion when she would return but couldn't bring herself to order the housekeeper to close the house.

Mrs. Green opened the door to the adjoining room. Cassie continued her tour. Lavette followed her into the bedroom. The same glorious light flooded this room. Cassie fingered the duvet on the four-poster bed. The snowy-white background edged in a pink flower and blue ribbon pattern made it the most beautiful she had ever seen.

"If there is anything else you need, my lady, please ring." Mrs. Green gestured at the wide tapestry bell pull that lay against the wall before taking her leave.

"Il est tres charmant, n'est-ce pas?" The French maid sighed with a silly smile plastered to her face.

Cassie removed her spencer and faced Lavette. "Yes, he is quite charming." *And certainly pleasant.* She felt numb. Too much was happening too fast.

Was it the extended time apart from the Stewart family and the sudden reunion that caused her uneasiness? Was it the squire ordering her about? Was it her uncertainty about her future husband?

Husband. That was an unsettling thought. Marriage to Edward appeared to be the only way she could get what she wanted. Cassie would do whatever it took to save her home, even if it meant tolerating the squire and his edicts, even if it meant marrying Edward.

Edward . . . she wondered. Undoubtedly, he must be very popular with the ladies. Cassie could see the effect his manner had on her maid, Lavette. There was no doubt. Edward Stewart was quite handsome. What woman would not want his attention? She should have felt fortunate that she was to marry him. Matters could have been much worse. Cassie's father might have insisted she marry the elder brother Julian.

Chapter Three

Edward Stewart entered through the open double doors of the library. "Good morning, Julian," he said with a quality that almost lent the greeting to music.

"I see that it is, isn't it?" The squire peered over his wire-rimmed eyeglasses at his jubilant younger brother.

"It is a perfect morning." Edward inhaled deep and opened his arms wide, greeting the warm rays of the sun. "Except, I do have a complaint, albeit a small one."

"Only one? Then it would seem far from perfect, would it not? What complaint do you have?"

"It's the valet, Valentine, is that his name? He seems a bit on the odd side, don't you think?"

"Odd? Hadn't noticed really." The only concern Julian had regarding staff came when the household did not run efficiently. He saw nothing that would indicate that such was the case.

"Well, it doesn't matter, really." Edward shrugged.

"What do you mean it doesn't matter?" The current valet saw to the squire's wardrobe and did an adequate job. "The fact that you bring up his name warrants discussion."

"He'll be gone in a fortnight. You'll chase him away just as you have all the others." Edward took a coffee cup and dispensed the steaming black liquid from the large silver urn on the credenza. "It's always the same. The capable valet I've hired has always gone by the time I return.

"You, dear brother, manage to fill the position. However I always find the cove you've hired, on the whole, unsuitable. Then I have to search for an adequate replacement. Then the process starts again. I do wish you'd let me have my own man."

"As I've explained before, Edward, we are not the aristocracy and as such we should not be expected to follow what they dictate as the latest fashion."

"It's not as if you haven't got the blunt." That off-the-cuff remark would get Edward nowhere. In a more restrained voice he continued. "I am representing the family when I travel for business. And as such I should not have to rely upon the local accommodations to supply me with some servant they simply have on hand."

"The one valet has enough to do when you are home. If we had two . . . I daresay, what would keep the two of them occupied?"

Edward did have an answer. "Like I said, I have only the one complaint. Otherwise it is the beginning of a glorious day."

"Perhaps you can enlighten me as to what makes this particular morning any more glorious than the others?" Julian straightened in his chair and set down his pen. Experience told him only a female could cause this type of euphoric behavior in his brother. The squire leaned back in his chair, giving Edward his undivided attention.

"I just met my bride-to-be upstairs. I believe my luck has continued to hold. Not only does her dowry promise to be sizable, but she is a beauty as well."

"What do you know of her dowry?" Julian said nothing more to his brother than what he'd needed to know.

Edward seated himself on the sofa and unceremoniously propped his feet up on the expensive table. "Perhaps I will hire my own man."

Edward sighed in exasperation and turned to Julian. "My dear brother, you know as well as I do that Cass is the only daughter of the Earl of Thaddbury. It's no secret, Lord Thadburry was a wealthy man."

"That is true," Julian agreed.

"And although his title and holding have gone to his heir, I do not believe he would have left his beloved daughter without a feather to fly with." Edward sipped his coffee and took a moment to savor the flavor. "I may not have the financial sense that you possess, dear brother. However I am not so blind that I cannot work that much out for myself. I'll tell you what else I suspect." He sat forward to address his elder sibling. "I know our father was at one time very good friends with the earl. For as long as I can recall it was understood our fathers had arranged for a marriage between our families."

Julian knew his brother had the facts correct but wasn't about to confirm or deny any of the details.

"Father had already seen to your marriage—it had been arranged before I'd been born, I believe. The fact that it didn't last long is no fault of yours. She'd always been a sickly girl." Edward's unpleasant expression subsided. "However, when it comes to Cass and me, neither of our fathers are around now but"—he motioned to Julian—"that's where you come in. You'll see to it that everyone is all right and tight, doing the proper thing. I wager that Cass' father was so adamant that she and I should marry, if she refuses to go through with it, she'll inherit nothing."

The squire would allow Edward his speculation about the details surrounding his upcoming nuptials. "And what may I ask do you hope to gain by this?" Julian had half-expected his brother to be unwilling to take the marital step.

"I don't need to be threatened by financial ruin. I

have you to bully me into marriage." Edward stood, walked toward Julian, and laughed. "However, I'd imagine there would be an increase in my quarterly allowance and a decrease in my workload."

"Less work you say?" Julian raised his eyebrows.

"It's not what I would wish for, mind. But I do think it's about time I settle down and think about filling the nursery. My providing an heir will take the pressure off you to remarry."

"We need not concern ourselves with providing an heir. We have no titles to pass on."

Edward set his hands on the desk and leaned in toward his brother. "But we have land and money I'm sure you'd like to see kept in the family."

Julian removed his spectacles, laying them to rest on his papers. "I suppose I should find a capable agent to fill your shoes. But you shouldn't allow that to concern you."

"It's the family business, of course it concerns me." Edward returned to his chair and once again propped his feet on the table. "Cass and I shall move to her beloved Hedgeway Park after we're wed. After we're settled and start our family, I can resume my activities."

"Lady Cassandra may still feel reluctant about the marriage, even with all you believe she stands to lose." Julian touched his recently assaulted cheek, recalling her objection.

Edward's smile faded. His boots made a resounding

thud from their resting position as he stood. "Why? Am I so horrible that she would not have me?" Edward splayed a hand upon his chest, offended by the mere suggestion.

"Do not take offense," the squire replied. "I do not believe it is a personal dislike. She did not say precisely, but I'm sure she has some foolish woman's notion of marrying without love and other such nonsense."

"Nonsense? Nonsense to you, older brother, but you must understand the desires of the fairer sex." Edward's words heated with every passing phrase. "One must be able to interpret their wishes, dreams and needs. You must fill their yearning, nurture their affection."

Julian remained unmoved by the lecture and lifted his hand to halt the verbal onslaught. "I'll leave the romantic pursuit entirely to you." He donned his spectacles and adjusted the circular frames to sit comfortably over his nose. "I agree that your talents lie in that area. I am quite sure that you would know better than I when it comes to love. If you feel you must win her heart then I wish you luck in doing so."

Edward accepted the challenge. His green eyes sparkled in anticipation. He stood and in two strides reached the desk and set his cup and saucer on the desk. He leaned toward Julian, catching his brother's eye. "You'll see, I'll have her completely dizzy in love with me," Edward stated in complete confidence.

"I would not underestimate her," the squire cautioned. "She appears very strong-willed. She might forego her inheritance to marry the man she loves."

"You shall see, Julian. I shall be that man! I shall win her love!"

A small harrumph came from the squire. He watched his younger brother bound out of the library doors, exhibiting a type of exuberance Julian found quite annoying.

He wondered how much of Edward's babbling about the foolishness of love was true, then grumbled at his brother's carelessness when he spotted Edward's discarded cup and saucer on the corner of his desk. With a huff, the squire moved the ill-deposited set to a side table, where it would be out of his way, and returned to his work.

Dressed in a dark gray mourning gown, Lady Cassandra emerged from the first-story landing and descended the stairs. From down the hall Edward approached with arms outstretched to greet her.

"Cass, you will allow me the great pleasure of showing you Stewart Hall." Edward pulled her arm through his, resting her hand upon his arm, and placed his hand atop hers.

"I don't really see how I can refuse." Her awkward reply indicated that she'd been caught off guard. Perhaps she feared that if she declined, it might sound less than cordial.

She glanced, quite by accident, to the squire watching the proceedings from just outside the library doors. Lady Cassandra did not smile.

Julian wondered if Edward's efforts to win her affections were in vain. The squire watched Edward continue to ramble, leading her down the corridor toward the Gallery at the far end of the house.

"We shan't tour the entire house. Not only would it be a considerable undertaking, I'm afraid we haven't time for it at the present." Edward's smile was infectious. The squire had no doubt that her mood would lighten as all women seemed to do when sharing his company. "We must leave something for us to look forward to, mustn't we?"

Cassie took note of the comments Edward made about the history of the family and the house. There were more than just a few times she caught her guide's inspecting gaze come her way.

Edward conducted himself with such resplendent mode and bearing. He treated Cassie with the utmost respect and he was all that was gentlemanly.

Cassie found him pleasant. He was very charming and it wasn't long before she found her spirits beginning to lighten. The sides of her mouth began to turn upward. Then she smiled.

Not a full, wide smile by any means. Not at first. Then to her surprise, her smile was followed shortly by a laugh. Whatever magic Edward had woven, it had worked by the time they finished his brief tour.

Removing to the rear gardens, Cassie noted the overcast morning that had accompanied her to this grand house had given way to a moderately warm afternoon. The sun cleared any trace of mist that had the slightest thought of remaining throughout the day.

"You see, back in the seventeenth century Stewart Hall was a good half day's travel from town," Edward explained. "Now a scant two hundred years later we find London fairly upon our doorstep. However, if one retreats to the rear of the house . . ."

He led Cassie down a wide path and through a maze of low box hedges. She admired the flower beds within the hedges that supplied a stunning variety of colors. As she passed the pond in the garden, stray droplets misplaced by the wind threatened to shower her. She passed the rose bushes and stood on a large grass area that spread from the estate toward the outer edge of the countryside. As far as she could see was open and unplanted land.

"When one retreats into the rear gardens," Edward explained, "one could fool one's self by believing they were deep in the country."

"That's amazing." The landscape reminded Cassie quite a lot of Hedgeway Park.

"Julian won't even consider having a townhouse when we are so close."

A faint sound of barking caught Cassie's attention. A female figure in white crossed the vast green stretch of grass. A long, flowing pink veil streamed from a narrow-brimmed straw hat which matched the pink bandeau of her dress. She could only be Lorna, the only sister of the Stewart brothers.

Lorna's delicate laughter laced the air as she romped with Romeo. As soon as Romeo noticed his owner, he ran toward Cassie. Once receiving her greeting, he turned and dashed back down the lawn to his new playmate.

It took only Edward's approach to bring a wider smile to his sister's lips. "Good afternoon, Lorna."

"And to you, Edward." Lorna looked at Cassie with a hint of recognition. "Isn't he adorable?" Lorna gushed, petting the brown and white terrier.

"Yes," Edward acknowledged, his tone indifferent. "Quite the canine." A polite smile graced his lips. "Lady Cassandra, may I introduce my sister Miss Lorna Stewart."

"Now, I remember you! Lady Cassandra!"

"You weren't more than four or five when my father and I moved away," Cassie said. "You've grown into a beautiful young lady."

"I've just had my come out three weeks ago," Lorna noted with pride. "I remember looking up to you *so* when I was little."

"There is no need now. Both you lovely ladies will be the envy of London."

She and Lorna turned toward one another. Giggles erupted although Cassie tried her best to prevent the silliness from escaping.

Lorna turned to the terrier. "And who might this be?"

"That is Romeo." Cassie clapped her hands and he came running to her side.

"He is most delightful!" Lorna bent to pat him.

The butler appeared behind Edward. "I'm sorry to disturb you, sir."

"What is it, Maxwell?"

"The squire wishes for me to remind you of your up-coming commitment." The butler's face never hinted of an expression.

"Dash it all! That meeting with Farthington!" Edward slapped his forehead with the palm of his hand. He turned toward the ladies and gave a rueful sigh. "It completely escaped me! Maxwell, have my horse brought 'round front"—and he threw over his shoulder—"tell my brother I'll be on my way presently."

"Very well, sir," Maxwell acknowledged with the slightest inclination of his head. In a thrice he was gone.

"I am most frightfully sorry." Edward took Cassie's hand. "Although I might blame my lapse of memory on you." He smiled, exuding tremendous charm. "Your enchanting presence caused the entire matter to leave my mind completely. Julian becomes quite intolerable when it comes to business—won't accept any excuses. I fear I must take leave of you both."

Edward bent over Cassie's hand and stroked the

smooth skin on the back of her hand with his thumb. It was too intimate a gesture, too soon.

"I promise to do my utmost to make amends at the ball tomorrow night for my premature departure today."

"It will be such fun with you along," Lorna gushed with exuberance.

"*Where* are we going?" This was the first Cassie had heard of any festivities.

"Lord and Lady Addison's," Lorna said with a great deal of excitement. "Oh, but you must come with us."

"I don't think I have anything appropriate to wear."

"You must have something . . . I've got dozens of new gowns . . . you might . . ." Lorna trailed off and whatever thought might have crossed her mind at that moment was lost.

Edward glanced at the drab dress that hung loosely on Cassie with a quizzical eye that said that he was not quite sure what lay beneath. She could feel his attention linger on her for a longer period than she felt he needed.

"On second thought, I don't think any of mine will do," Lorna decided after a lengthy, measuring gaze.

Cassie's wardrobe consisted only of an assortment of half-mourning dresses and a few dark-colored gowns.

"Well then, we must take you shopping," Lorna

announced. "You must have several dancing gowns—
and day dresses, morning gowns, and riding habits . . .
and so much more. Also you'll need all sorts of
matching bonnets, slippers, and gloves." She ran out
of breath. "Of course, they all could not possibly be
ready in time for tomorrow, but I'm sure we could
manage to find you a gown or two. Oh, how I do adore
shopping."

"Much to our older brother's dismay." Edward's
gaze swung to his sister, looking at her from the corner
of his eye. He chuckled. Turning to Cassie, he raised
her hand for a final farewell before retreating toward
the main house.

Edward traipsed over the gray pea-pebbled path
with light steps as if airborne. Romeo followed at his
heels with an occasional nip at his trouser leg. Edward
frowned and glanced downward.

He shook his leg from the jaws of Cassie's playful
pet and mumbled an audible, "Mongrel." Halfway
there, Edward spun in midair for a last look. He nodded at the ladies, sporting a captivating smile.

"I don't think I've ever seen him so happy." Lorna
smiled. Edward disappeared into the back of the
house. "I believe it is all due to you!"

"I'm sure I cannot take all the credit." Cassie
watched Romeo scamper from the house toward her.
He slid to a halt and faced the mansion.

"Missy!" a shrill voice called out. "Miss-ssey!" it
called even louder. The terrier's ears swiveled forward,

standing alert, waiting for someone to approach from the house.

Lorna did not answer but turned toward Cassie. "You'll excuse Mrs. Upton's manners, won't you?" By the tone of Lorna's voice Cassie surmised the two ladies shared a somewhat adversarial relationship. "She's a bit unconventional for one in her position, but she has been with me for as long as I can remember."

Mrs. Upton came through the door and approached the garden. She glanced downward, her lips moved as she cursed under her breath. Holding the hem of her skirt up to avoid touching the ground, she made her way to Lorna and Cassie.

"Lady Cassandra." Lorna turned to the older woman. "This is Mrs. Upton, my companion."

"Not hardly—your governess more like," Mrs. Upton corrected without missing a beat.

"Fustian, I'm too old for a governess," the young miss snapped back. Romeo leaped up to remind Lorna of his omission from her proper introductions. "I'm sorry. This is Romeo, Lady Cassandra's pet."

Mrs. Upton turned a cold eye toward the dog, ignoring him, and welcomed Cassie with a polite curtsy. "Very pleased to meet you, my lady. You are Mr. Edward's intended, are you not?"

"I suppose . . . yes, I am." Cassie found Mrs. Upton's address shocking to say the least. However, she could see how the friendly bantering between the pair of them kept Lorna amused.

"Mr. Edward is such a wonderful young man." Mrs. Upton winked. "You are very fortunate. I believe he is a great favorite of the ladies," she whispered from the corner of her mouth.

"I think there have been at least a dozen broken hearts since your betrothal announcement." Lorna sighed.

"That's enough, young lady. We can gossip over our tea inside." Mrs. Upton urged her toward the house. "Mrs. Green will have tea set up in the front parlor. We'd best not keep her waiting." Mrs. Upton trailed behind with her skirts in hand and called out to quicken the pace. "Come along, now, the both of you. If we dally any longer, it will get cold!"

Chapter Four

Once inside the house, Cassie followed Lorna into the front parlor and sat next to her on the striped sofa. Romeo trotted in and sat next to the table. Lorna took a biscuit, broke a piece off, and offered it to him.

"Where are your manners, child?" The governess swiped at Lorna's generous hand.

"Cassie doesn't mind," she replied in a brazen tone.

Mrs. Upton poured the tea, wrinkled her nose at her charge, and said nothing.

Cassie suspected this young Stewart woman would continue to push the limits of etiquette. One would hope not so far as to make herself a social outcast. That would not do at all, not with the squire as guardian. No doubt he corrected her every improper move.

"We need to see Madam Bosqué when we have finished," Lorna announced once she sat. "I'm sure the modiste will manage to find you a gown or two."

"Two?" Mrs. Upton grumbled and cast her charge a stern look. "Three, more like, perhaps four."

"Oh, very well, four. Madam Bosqué always makes my gowns and I do believe she might be persuaded to provide you with something beautiful to wear for tomorrow evening."

"If she knows which side her bread is buttered on, she will." Mrs. Upton set her cup and saucer aside and stood. "I'll send a footman 'round to fetch her. I'm sure you'll have your choice of gowns."

"Surely she would prefer if I visited the shop." Cassie did not wish to disturb anyone, not even a dressmaker.

"But you've only arrived. Are you not fatigued?" Lorna narrowed her eyes in concentration over her Sèvres cup.

Cassie didn't have to think about that answer. She was exhausted.

"If she knows what's good for her she'll come running *tout de suite*," Mrs. Upton said before leaving the room.

Madam Bosqué and her assistant Madeleine arrived at Stewart Hall before the three ladies had finished with tea. They were led into a side parlor and it became a makeshift salon for their use. There, Madam Bosqué and Lorna made suggestions about color and style choices for Cassie, conforming to the latest fashions. The modiste brought with her several pre-made dresses that she could easily alter and could be made ready to wear by tomorrow evening.

While Madam Bosqué marked the gowns for alterations, Lorna went on to tell Cassie of the wonderful balls and assemblies she had missed since the beginning of the season.

Lorna wanted to introduce her best friend Belinda Hastings. They were of the same age and got along so famously, it was not to be believed. They conversed on all the important subjects such as dresses, parties, and men, dancing slippers, balls, and oh, yes, men.

"We shall have the most extraordinary time tonight," Lorna told Cassie. "Belinda and I have already decided who we shall marry. I will wed the Honorable Jeffery Rutherford and Belinda—"

"It doesn't do for you to set your cap on some young gentleman," Mrs. Upton scolded her charge. "I think you might do best to ask the squire his permission first."

Lorna ignored her governess and continued. "Belinda adores my brother, Edward. Although he is all that is kind to her, I have informed her many times that he is quite out of her reach and she must choose another. We have agreed that she might make an amiable match with Jeffery's very good friend Thomas Wentworth."

Lorna paid particular attention that she had not omitted any descriptions of the especially handsome men who had made her acquaintance. She spoke in particular detail about the ones that captured her capricious fancy, much to the horror of Mrs. Upton.

"Ze blue, is she not *tres belle*, Mademoiselle Lorna?" Madam Bosqué stepped back, admiring her work.

Cassie gazed at her reflection in the full-length glass that had been brought to the small parlor for their use. She hardly recognized herself in a gown that fit, and it was a shade of blue that brought out the color of her eyes. It had been so long since she'd worn anything besides gray.

"Someday, I hope to marry someone as dashing as my brother, Edward," Lorna told Cassie. "Even if I found him now, Julian would never permit me to marry nor would he tolerate a serious involvement. It's only my first season, you know."

"I would hope not!" Mrs. Upton reeled at the girl's implication.

Madam Bosqué and her assistant ushered Cassie away and helped her disrobe, careful not to allow the straight pins to stick her.

Cassie returned in a cream-colored gown, the second gown they all agreed she would have altered for tomorrow's ball. She took her place in front of the mirror to be fitted. Lorna proceeded with her discourse.

"We haven't a title but our wealth and land seem to have blinded society. I think he's terrified I might form a *tendre* for a fortune hunter. Julian's already told me that I am to have my heart's desire. As long as he's suitable." Lorna drew herself back and continued with reserve. "He said making an immediate match wouldn't be a *prudent* thing to do."

I'm sure he did. Cassie could just imagine it would be the exact words the squire, acting in his position as dutiful guardian, would utter.

At dinner later that evening, Cassie would almost have enjoyed the quiet except that Squire Stewart was seated at the head of the massive table. He and Lorna displayed healthy appetites, making their portions of ham and vegetables disappear.

Cassie found the succulent repast could not tempt her. The new surroundings were pleasant but the company was not—*he* was there. She managed to keep herself busy by cutting her boiled carrots into small pieces and arranging them from one side of her plate to the other, not tasting a morsel.

The squire might have noticed Cassie's lack of interest in her dinner the few times he'd glanced in her direction but he never bothered to inquire. She thought it quite possible that he never noticed that she was not eating nor ever wondered why.

Was the food's temperature, aroma, or perhaps the appearance not to her liking? Could he possibly conceive of any other reason her dinner had remained untouched?

It had not, however, dissuaded him from finishing his. Laying his utensils to rest, he dropped his napkin next to his plate. "If you ladies will excuse me."

"Of course, Julian, do not let us keep you," Lorna said with a gracious nod. "I know that your work is calling for your attention."

"Thank you." He rose from the table, gave a slight bow, and left.

The squire's behavior bordered upon rude. However, his absence was welcome. Cassie could feel herself relax once he had vacated the room.

"Julian can be a bit intimidating." Lorna smiled across the table at Cassie.

"I don't find him intimidating at all." Cassie took a bite of carrot. "I just don't care for him." From what Cassie could observe, he hadn't treated Lorna with any more warmth than he had her. "I cannot imagine how you manage to be so cheerful when someone such as he is your example of decorum. I've never met a more uncaring, unfeeling, human being in my life."

"You make him sound positively odious." Lorna straightened, clearly upset by Cassie's forthright opinion.

"Pray, excuse me, I did not mean to offend you."

Cassie was sorry her words had hurt Lorna but she spoke the truth. "I do, however, beg that you prove me wrong."

"He does mean well," Lorna said in his defense then stared into her plate. "It is not his nature. He didn't . . . you just don't understand him."

Returning to her plate, Cassie cut into her meat as if it was his flesh. After causing sufficient injury to her entree, she set her utensils on the edge of the plate with a sense of satisfaction. Lifting her napkin, she dabbed each side of her mouth and remained seated until Lorna finished. She did not have to wait long.

After dinner, Cassie declined a game of cards, wishing only to be alone in the quiet and solitude of her room. Her first day at Stewart Hall had been long, very full, and emotionally draining.

Changing into her chemise, she drew on her robe and pulled it tight at the waist. She retrieved her book of Byron's poetry and moved to the settee near the crackling hearth, warming herself. Cassie read for ten minutes and found it impossible to keep her eyes open. Soon the book lowered and found its final resting place on her chest, just under her chin.

Cassie woke a bit disoriented the next morning. It took a few minutes of staring at the unfamiliar heavy, deep-red curtains of her four-poster bed to remember where she was and what she was doing there.

Despite what she had thought, despite what she had hoped, it had not been a dream.

"Finally, you have awoken! It eez such a beautiful morning!" Lavette entered with a breakfast tray and set it on the table near the bed. "I am told that you have several gowns arriving for ze ball *ce soir.*"

Cassie could manage only a nod. Lavette handed her a cup of chocolate.

"Mademoiselle Lorna *et* Romeo are in the *jardin.* I believe she loves ze little dog as much as you!"

And it was clear to Cassie that if Romeo did not feel the same for Lorna, he would not be spending so much time with her. Cassie smiled, remembering how the two of them were running across the back lawn yesterday. "They do enjoy one another's company, don't they?"

"You must dress and join them. The air, she eez good for the lungs." The maid pulled the untouched cup of chocolate from Cassie's hands.

"I really am not looking forward to facing the people below." Cassie slid her legs over the side of the bed. She hadn't meant everyone, just *him.*

"Everything, everyone eez new—we are strangers here. But you must not let them frighten you. *Votre père*—"

Yes, Cassie's father wanted this for her. But did he really? Losing her home, marrying a man she hardly knew, making near-strangers a part of her family cannot be what he truly wanted. She felt so miserable and unhappy while away from Hedgeway Park and the only way, it seemed, that she could return as its rightful owner was if she married Edward Stewart.

"—you must show zem you are not frightened of zem. Especially za squire." Lavette paused and her gaze met Cassie's. It was clear they shared the same opinion of him. They needn't say another word, they both understood quite well.

That horrid man.

Lavette was right, Cassie decided. She needed to show she wasn't afraid. Cassie intended to keep Hedgeway Park and she would do whatever was necessary—even if she had to put up with the squire. Marrying Edward would be the easy part.

"I am ready to dress." Cassie stood, regained possession of the cup of chocolate and headed for the dressing table.

The clinking of dishes and utensils attracted Cassie's attention upon her arrival downstairs. She approached the breakfast room to find Mrs. Upton watching the morning's fare being laid out on the sideboard.

"Ah, Lady Cassandra, good day to you." Mrs. Upton could not have sounded more pleasant. She gestured to the many serving dishes. "Have you had a chance to—"

"No, only chocolate in my room."

"Not to worry, the luncheon dishes will be out soon.

I suggest you have a hearty meal since you'll be attending the Addisons' ball tonight. Have you seen Miss Lorna about?"

"I believe she is in the rear garden with Romeo."

"Romeo?" The shock in the governess' voice was apparent as if Lorna shared company with an undesirable young man.

"Romeo is my pet terrier." Cassie hoped the explanation would belie any fears. "I am on my way out to see them now."

"Oh, yes, of course. When you see Miss Lorna, will you ask her to please return to the house?" Mrs. Upton collected two clean plates and set them on the table.

"I will be happy to relay your message."

Moving down the hall, she heard Mrs. Upton speak to herself. "At the break of dawn the girl nibbles on the corner a piece of toast with a sip of tea and thinks that's going to keep her until the ball tonight . . ."

Cassie smiled but that smile faded once she thought of continuing down the hall to the back door of the house. Perhaps part of maintaining a peaceful association with the squire meant avoiding him. She went out of her way to exit the house through the front door. Cassie walked around the far side of the house to avoid the library window and the squire who might be gazing from it.

The gravel path around the low box hedges ran the width of the house, past the fountain, toward the vast lawn where Lorna and Romeo roamed.

"La-dy Cass-an-dra!" Lorna cried out, waving from the expanse of lawn.

Cassie raised her hand, letting Lorna know she would be there directly. Lorna and Romeo approached, meeting Cassie halfway.

"Do not tell me you have been out here all morning." Cassie held her hand to her forehead, shielding her eyes from the sunlight.

"We have been having a most delightful time." Lorna sat on her heels, patting Romeo who seemed to devour the attention. "He is so wonderfully attentive and has boundless energy."

Much like the young woman who uttered those words. Cassie preferred the calm and sedate Romeo who slumbered by her side as she read or did needlework. In any case, it was Cassie's opinion that Romeo was a companionable canine who had a great deal of insight into humans and their nature.

"Mrs. Upton asked that you return to the house."

Lorna groaned then stood. "Doesn't she know that I am far too excited to eat?"

Cassie could not imagine how Lorna would remain standing for an entire day without nourishment. "Will your growling stomach embarrass you tonight?"

Lorna gazed at Cassie as if she had come up with the most brilliant observation imaginable. "You're absolutely right. I should have something to sustain me, shouldn't I?"

"They were getting ready to serve luncheon just as

I left." Cassie felt her own empty stomach beginning to protest.

"Let's be off then. I'm sure darling Romeo is famished!" Lorna motioned that they should all walk toward the house.

"Romeo is always famished," Cassie repeated and fell into step beside Lorna. "He should wait at the foot of the stairs until we have finished eating."

They reached the house and entered through the back door.

"Why?" Lorna protested. "I'd like him to sit right next to me at the table."

"It cannot be very pleasant for him to smell the food in the very same room and not be allowed a bite." Cassie wanted to inform her that being kind to him wasn't really being kind at all. "I'll wager he can still smell the meat from where he sits."

"I'll feed him tidbits from my very own plate."

"You'll spoil him." They stopped at the foot of the staircase. "He can wait right here. You may save whatever you like for him and when we've finished, you can give them to him on his own dish."

Lorna agreed. "I promise to save something extra special for you, Romeo."

"Remember," Cassie said to her dog, "you stay right there until we return." Romeo lowered himself to the floor, giving every indication that he was staying put.

The two empty plates Mrs. Upton had placed upon

the table waited for Cassie and Lorna. The sideboard stood brimming with various meats, vegetables, and other savories. All the dishes were overlooked when Lorna spotted two packages on the table before them. She opened the accompanying letter and scanned its contents.

"It's from Edward! He says, '*To My Dear Ladies, I would like to think you have been blue-deviled since my departure. However, I suspect my little rival has been keeping you two in high spirits and running you to near exhaustion throughout the countryside.*'" Lorna looked up at Cassie. "He must be referring to Romeo."

Lorna dropped the missive on the table and studied the parcels a bit closer. "This one's for me"—she pulled the package marked with an L closer—"and that one"—Lorna pointed at the remaining package, marked with a C—"is for you." With the letter set aside, she eagerly tore at the wrapping. "He is forever sending presents!"

"Is he?" Cassie wasn't used to receiving gifts unless there was a special occasion. She took up the letter to read the last bit.

I pray that his activity will not prevent you from our sharing a dance or two this evening. Please accept these gifts as a token of my affection.

Yr humble servant, E. Stewart

"Oh, it's beautiful." Lorna twirled the closed parasol, shaking the ruffles free from their confinement. Opening the Alice blue-colored parasol, Lorna set it to rest upon her shoulder where she made a slow turn to allow Cassie an unobtrusive view at her latest treasure. "Quick, open your package!"

Had Cassie not have moved swiftly enough, Lorna might have shred the wrapping from the remaining gift as well. The package had the same dimensions as Lorna's and it would have surprised Cassie if something other than a parasol lay within. She laid the letter on the table and unwrapped a dark rose-colored parasol.

"Isn't that lovely?" Lorna reached out to finger the ruffled edge. "Will that not match your new puce-colored walking dress?"

"Since I am not in possession of that dress it would be difficult to tell. I shall pen a 'thank you' after we finish our meal." Cassie thought that would be the proper thing to do.

"Goose. There is no need." Lorna laughed. "We shall see Edward tonight at the ball!"

Chapter Five

By the time Lorna had finished her meal, she had saved Romeo a considerable amount of food on a very small plate. Cassie had to insist he be limited to a morsel or two. If he was allowed to consume the entire plateful of food, not only would it make him ill but her once compliant pet would become irreversibly spoilt.

Thank goodness Lorna did not object. While she agonized over the choices, Romeo licked his chops with anticipation and Mrs. Upton descended the stairs behind them.

"Lady Cassandra, your gowns for tonight have just arrived. I saw your maid removing the tissue from the blue gown."

"Oh, let's do go see!" The news of Cassie's gowns

hastened Lorna's ability to decide on which tidbit to give Romeo.

Once he had swallowed the treats, without benefit of chewing, the three ascended the stairs toward Cassie's room.

"Oh, you came to zee for yourself!" Lavette wasted no time pulling out the newly arrived dresses. "Zee blue is *tres magnifique*! But zee *autre . . .*"

She pulled the lighter, cream silk satin from the wardrobe. The gown sparkled, even in the filtered bedroom light from the windows.

"You must wear this tonight," Lorna announced. "It is breathtaking!"

Madam Bosqué had gone far beyond what Cassie had expected. Not only had the modiste altered the dress to fit, she added delicate silver thread stitching and small, intricate beading at the neckline and bodice.

"It seems impossible that this is the same gown I slipped on yesterday." Cassie ran her fingers over the beading, admiring the workmanship.

"I told you Madam Bosqué was talented. I think she's quite outdone herself." Lorna's face beamed. "I cannot wait to see what Edward thinks of it!"

It was all Cassie could do to tolerate sitting in an enclosed area of a carriage with Squire Stewart. What made it tolerable was that he dressed entirely in black with the exception of his white shirt and cravat.

Cassie could almost imagine he was not there and that she and Lorna were riding alone to the ball.

Lord and Lady Addison resided in one of the large mansions that stood on the north side of Grovesner Square. Cassie and Lorna entered the residence with the squire. Jeffrey Rutherford, whom Cassie had recognized at once due to Lorna's lengthy and very accurate description of him, had been waiting near the entrance. Lorna took Jeffrey's arm and he led her off to meet with some of their friends.

Cassie was left standing alone with the squire. The situation did not last long and she was relieved to find that Edward was as good as his word. He arrived at the Addisons' residence only ten minutes after she had.

Her enthusiasm in seeing him had not so much to do with her heart growing fonder because of his absence, as much as he would be the one to remove her from the squire's company.

Upon laying eyes on her, Edward's mouth opened to comment but he was struck momentarily speechless. "The transformation is absolute!" he finally said. "I thought you radiant before but now you are a veritable vision in that gown." He took up her hand and bowed over it. "Is she not the most beautiful woman in this room, Julian?"

Cassie was relieved that the squire was nearsighted. She was spared the indignity of being spied at through a quizzing glass. He did turn his gaze upon her, perhaps for the first time all evening.

"You look quite fashionable, my lady." The squire accompanied his comment with a low bow.

Was fashionable meant as a compliment? Cassie hoped her displeasure did not show.

"I am certainly the luckiest man in attendance, if not the most fortunate man in all of England, to have you stand by my side." He took up Cassie's hand as if it was as precious and delicate as fine china.

She returned his smile—perhaps with less luster and more effort on her part. It surprised her how little his praise pleased her. It should have meant more but she was not so easily flattered. Cassie felt numb at the thought that Edward was the man she would be with for the rest of her life.

The squire cleared his throat. "If you both will excuse me."

"Julian, if you would stay for a moment. I have news"—Edward glanced at Cassie—"for you both."

The squire stepped forward, attentive.

"My recent meeting with Farthington precipitates my travel to the continent." Edward turned to his brother. "There's a letter for you and a copy of the contracts on your desk. I leave tomorrow for the coast." He turned to Cassie. "I can most honestly tell you how badly I feel about leaving."

"How long will you be away?" Cassie found the news disturbing.

"About a fortnight." Edward squeezed her hand. "Perhaps a bit longer."

"I best reply to Farthington and look over the details of the contract before you leave," the squire interrupted. "This is dashed inconvenient."

"Julian—language, please!" Edward scolded.

The squire glanced at Cassie. "I beg your pardon," he said with a nod. "I wish I had time to find someone to take your place. You should be here attending to your intended."

"As it is, I must go. If you desire to keep our business dealings within the family, you might want to look to Mr. Rutherford, there." Edward nodded toward the young man standing next to their sister. "He looks to be well on his way to joining us, wouldn't you say?"

The squire stared into the crowd. "We'll just see about this." He stalked away in Lorna's direction and muttered, "That undisciplined young pup!"

Edward's laughter ebbed. "My absence may be for the best. I only say this because of the circumstance you find yourself in. I cannot imagine this is the life you've envisioned for yourself. As for me"—a glorious smile broke across his face—"just because our marriage was arranged does not make it any less desirable."

Cassie wished she could have felt the same type of infatuation as he. It would have made their situation much easier to accept. At the moment she could think of him only in kind regard.

"If only our fathers were here to enjoy our celebration. I think seeing us unite our families would have made them very happy."

"I suppose you are correct. I know our fathers were once close and I knew of my father's wish. I thought it was a dream he wanted to witness. Once he fell ill I imagined he had given up on seeing our families joined. Now that he's passed . . . I never considered he would insist upon us marrying, even from his grave."

"I suggest we take the little time we have tonight and see what events might come our way—separation and all." Edward's soft voice, filled with kindness and understanding, seemed to ease Cassie's fears. "Although you are not exactly a stranger, you have been displaced—away from your friends and your home. There will be time enough for us to become acquainted when I return. Can we simply enjoy this evening and not concern ourselves with what is to come?"

Somehow his suggestion made Cassie feel better. Not only was Edward attentive to her throughout the evening, he kept a protective eye on his sister as well.

It was quite apparent to Cassie that Lorna did not need Edward looking after her. The squire did not allow any young bucks to linger at Miss Stewart's side. A gentleman might desire a second dance, as was the case with Jeffrey Rutherford, but none was to be had.

Edward, who had two dances with Cassie, made

sure she enjoyed herself immensely and was partnered for every set.

All in all, it was a wonderful evening.

Cassie made sure to rise early the next morning so as not to miss Edward's departure.

"You needn't see me off," he remarked. "But I am happy you did." He kissed her hand and placed it in the crook of his arm then led the way to the breakfast room. "I do have a slight concern . . . I hesitate to bring up the matter."

"Please, say what is on your mind, I am most willing to do what I can to put you at ease." Cassie stood her ground, causing Edward to stop.

"Am I correct in assuming that you and Julian do not rub along well together?"

She felt as if he was accusing her. "I can hardly take the blame. I was not the one who demanded I present myself at Stewart Hall. Nor was I the one who foisted myself onto your family." Cassie softened her voice to add, "You and Miss Lorna have been all that is pleasant, the squire however has not—it does not signify."

"You've taken a dislike to him, then?" Edward certainly felt strongly about his brother, as did Lorna.

"I do not know him well enough to truly dislike him."

"You simply do not understand Julian."

"Your sister said the very same thing to me. Could

you please tell me what that means? Pray, exactly what do I not understand?"

"Julian is not—" Edward reconsidered his words. "Well, he has some very good qualities."

"Such as . . ." Cassie would be more than willing to give the squire a chance to redeem himself. He'd barely said ten words to her since that first day.

"He's got an uncompromising sense of duty and morality," Edward said optimistically.

"And?"

"And . . ." Edward searched for other positive traits. "He's very punctual."

"Punctual? Is that the most you can say to recommend him? He's punctual?"

"I am at a loss at the moment. Forgive me." Edward, still escorting Cassie, continued to the breakfast room. They nearly collided with the squire and Maxwell who were on their way out. "Julian, a moment of your time. If you will be seated."

When Edward would brook no protest, Julian returned to his seat and Maxwell stood at his side.

"We are supposed to be family." Edward glanced from Lady Cassandra to Julian. "Just as I am on my way out of the country I learn that my betrothed and my brother cannot stand the sight of one another."

"That is a bit harsh, Edward. Nothing of the sort is going on." It was not Julian's place to entertain his brother's bride. Had he not seen to her welfare? Provided a new wardrobe for her since she'd just come out of mourning?

Julian looked at Lady Cassandra. Had she been filling Edward's mind with lies?

"I want the two of you to come together—at least be civil . . . for my benefit if nothing else." Edward's stern tone kept their attention. "The two of you *will* make an effort to behave in a well-mannered fashion toward one another. Every morning you are to exchange a pleasantry over this very table." Edward drove his index finger into its surface with a resounding thump. "Maxwell, you will bear witness to this—every morning of my absence, I say!"

"Sir, I—" Maxwell did not have a chance to accept or refuse.

"And Julian, as head of the family I expect you to make the first overture."

"As you wish. I will do as you ask." There was no good reason he should refuse such a simple request.

"Good. My lady?" Edward looked at Lady Cassandra.

"Yes, of course. I shall comply." Her pleasant tone might have gladly accepted Edward's request but at the same time the squire could hear the disdain she held for him.

"If, upon my return, you two have developed an all-consuming affection for the other, well . . . it could not please me more." Edward bid them farewell and kissed

Lady Cassandra's hand before leaving the squire in the breakfast room with *her.*

The very next morning, Maxwell observed the squire waiting at the breakfast table until Lady Cassandra's arrival. He stood as she entered the room and greeted her with, "Good morning, my lady."

"Good day to you, sir."

With a polite bow, the squire left. Lady Cassandra sat at the table after helping herself to a cup of coffee and a piece of toast from the sideboard.

The butler thought the first exchange, although strained, was a good beginning on both behalves.

The second morning of Mr. Edward's absence, Squire Stewart rose from the table as Lady Cassandra entered the room and said, "Good day to you, my lady."

Lady Cassandra returned his sentiment with, "I bid you good morning, sir."

The squire then vacated the room, leaving Lady Cassandra to breakfast with her coffee and toast.

On the third day, Maxwell noted a change. The squire rose from the table as always when Lady Cassandra entered the room. In a cordial but unenthusiastic fashion, he said to her, "Good morning, Lady Cassandra."

"Good day to you, sir."

"I wish you a pleasant day."

"How kind of you, sir. May you have a productive day as well."

The squire left and headed for the study. Lady Cassandra remained, with her coffee and toast as her only company.

After witnessing this morning's tepid exchange, Maxwell thought it might be beneficial for the family's welfare if they proceeded beyond simple conversation.

"Excuse me, sir." Maxwell approached the squire that evening in his study.

"What is it, Maxwell?" The squire did not look up from the papers before him.

"Lady Cassandra, sir."

Squire Stewart shot to his feet, dropping the pen onto the desk. "Is she here?" He looked past the butler to the doorway, where she might be waiting to have a moment with him. The squire's first encounter with her, just outside this room, must have been as memorable for him as it had been for Maxwell.

"No, I believe she has retired for the night."

At those words the squire seemed to relax and regained his seat. "Well, then, what is it . . . that concerns Lady Cassandra?"

"It was Mr. Edward's wish that his new family should—for lack of a better word—*warm* to one another. He asked that you begin by exchanging pleasantries."

"It is no easy task for me, Maxwell. I can't tell you

how it feels to wake and know that I have to face her every morning . . . the woman can't abide me."

"I only wish to mention that Lady Cassandra has no acquaintances here in town. Her only constant human companionship is that of Miss Lorna, who is not quite, shall we say, an equal?"

"Lorna's a silly little thing." The squire chuckled with a smile. "I shouldn't think anyone at that age could cope with Lady Cassandra's current difficulties." He eased back in his chair and reflected. "An arranged marriage can be most challenging. It does not always work out for the best. I was a most fortunate man."

Maxwell recalled the squire's venture into matrimony which had him leg-shackled to a pleasant but ordinary daughter of a viscount, a friend of the previous squire's. Both were content with the match but neither party was overjoyed to be with their chosen spouse.

Such was the way of an arranged marriage.

"I believe Lady Cassandra has every intention of respecting her father's wishes and will marry Mr. Edward. Most couples in their position are somewhat discontent. I do not believe this is the case here. From what I have observed, she and Mr. Edward have an *understanding.*"

The squire stared, with great interest, toward Maxwell.

"Their difficulty lies with—I beg your pardon, sir—*you.*"

"Me?" The squire looked affronted.

"Although she finds her betrothal amiable, it is quite clear that Lady Cassandra harbors some residual resentment toward you."

"It is my responsibility to carry out her father's wishes, whether it be tallying the quarterly expenses or paying for her dancing slippers."

"Yes, sir, and you have done so admirably since the earl's death. Nevertheless, she does not look upon you kindly." Maxwell tried his best to express his sympathy. "Before his absence, Mr. Edward made it clear that he wishes to resolve the discord within his family. Furthermore, I believe you have succeeded."

"Why, thank you, Maxwell."

"What better reception could Mr. Edward have than to see you and Lady Cassandra welcome him home side by side?"

The squire's eyes grew wide as he considered the notion.

"To this end, if Lady Cassandra were to acquaint herself with you"—Maxwell hoped the squire, who was not a feckless man, would catch on—"spend time with you and you with her, it may benefit you both."

"What would we do, Maxwell?" The squire had, clearly, spent too many years locked up in the study, alone, busy with his work and correspondence. He was far more comfortable with a full ink bottle and a pile of work papers.

"I should not think it inappropriate if you, as her

impending new family member, offered to accompany her for a daily activity—such as a stroll through the gardens, a drive through the park, or a morning ride."

A light flared behind the squire's eyes. "Brilliant suggestion," he shouted. "Maxwell, you're a genius!"

"Thank you, sir." The butler bowed and concealed his smile.

Chapter Six

The next morning, Julian sat at the breakfast table as he had the three previous mornings, waiting for Lady Cassandra's arrival. He stood when she entered the room.

"Good morning, Lady Cassandra."

"A good morning to you as well, Squire," she returned with a ring of finality.

He did not move to leave. "Would you mind if I remained and took coffee with you?"

She froze in the doorway. "I . . . that would be . . . by all means, stay. I welcome your company."

Julian returned to his seat.

"I thought"—Julian found that words were not coming easily to him—"that is to say . . . you spend a great deal of time with my sister."

"Miss Lorna is excellent company as well as very entertaining."

"However, in the mornings you are—" He paused.

"Lorna does not wake until noon," they said at the same time.

Quiet mirth eased the tension between them and they both offered shy, polite smiles.

He began again. "We have a fine stable." Or so he was told. Julian didn't ride much.

"Lorna does not ride," they said, again, at the same time. It seemed they both knew Lorna's habits quite well.

"Exactly," he said. "I thought that . . . well, since you are an early riser, as I am"—he wondered what he would say next—"and as we both are not occupied at this hour of the morning, or so it would seem, except for taking coffee"—he glanced from his cup to her—"I thought perhaps"—he paused again—"I thought we might go out riding together one morning," he blurted out at the same time she said, "I can't very well head out on my own."

"Excuse me?" Lady Cassandra set her cup and saucer on the table.

"I said, I would be delighted to accompany you," he repeated more bravely this time. "If you would care to do so." Then he added, "At the time of your choosing, of course."

She blinked and turned her head, looking at him out

of the corner of her eye as if she did not trust him. "I shall think on the matter, if that is agreeable to you."

Julian stood, preparing himself to leave the room. "You have only to ask, my lady." He bowed and left.

Cassie wondered what had come over the squire. This morning's conversation went beyond mere pleasantries. Offering to accompany her on a morning ride? She had thought he was quite indifferent to her. Then she thought that perhaps she ought to attempt to understand Squire Stewart, for Edward's sake.

It wasn't until that afternoon, when she and Lorna sat in the two tapestry-covered chairs by the hearth with needlework in hand, that she was able to put those disturbing thoughts aside. Mrs. Upton sat in the matching solid-colored sofa reading but not oblivious to the younger ladies in the room.

"Whatever shall I do?" Lorna sighed. "I've received permission to waltz at Almack's and I wanted my first to be with Edward."

"That is disappointing." Cassie drew her needle and pulled the thread taut. "I suppose in his absence your other brother will have to do."

"Do? He won't *do* at all, I'm afraid." Lorna sighed, disappointed with the situation.

"I admit that the squire is not Edward but I suppose you'll just have to make the best of it."

Lorna's hands came to a stop and dropped the needlework into her lap. She glared at Cassie with exasperation.

"Miss Lorna is despondent in losing her prestigious dance partner," Mrs. Upton clarified. "It has always been her dream that her first waltz would be with Mr. Edward."

"You have little choice, Lorna. I'm sure the squire will do his utmost to fill Edward's shoes." Cassie did not see any way around the problem.

"Fill his shoes? My dear, he can't possibly!" The governess chuckled, folding her book closed in her lap. "Squire Stewart cannot dance!"

"What's that you say?"

"Didn't you know? Julian can't dance." Lorna repeated. "Did you not notice last evening at the Addisons' ball? Not once did he step onto the dance floor."

Cassie could not recall seeing the squire partake in any of the dances. She smiled at the exposed minor imperfection of Squire Stewart. "Imagine not knowing how to dance in this day and age."

"There's no need really. It's not as if he enjoys social affairs." Mrs. Upton went on. "The squire learned the minuet so he could dance at his wedding but that was ages ago."

"I see." A hint of a smile threatened to betray her. *How very odd he is.* Even in Yorkshire, most of the farmers had the simple skill of leading a lady across the floor to music.

"I wouldn't worry, Lorna. I'm sure everything will work out."

"There will be plenty of young men there. You'll have your chance at a waltz." Mrs. Upton saw no reason to panic. She opened the book to where she had left off.

"I was really looking forward to waltzing with Edward first." Lorna sighed heavily, deeply.

Cassie knew how much Lorna worshipped him and could wholeheartedly sympathize with her. And truth be told, Cassie missed Edward's kindness and smiling face too.

Edward had been gone for nearly a week. The exchange in the breakfast room between Cassie and the squire that morning had been unremarkable. Why had she ever agreed to this folly of Edward's? It felt silly, almost comical, that the start of every day should begin with her and the squire trying to make meaningless conversation.

Day after day he greeted her with a banal salutation. And day after day she countered with a polite but equally absurd reply.

Cassie had promised to cooperate and so had the squire. As much as she disliked it and no matter what her opinion of this action, she understood they would continue in this fashion until Edward's return.

Cassie wondered, if only for a moment, if she ought to have accepted the squire's offer to accompany her for a morning ride. It would certainly be a pleasant way to start the day.

At three o'clock in the afternoon, Cassie glanced around, looking for Romeo. He was nowhere to be found. She walked to the far side of her sitting room. In one swift movement, she parted the sheers and her eyes began to search for the slightest movement of her terrier in the rear gardens. There was not a trace of him.

She turned away from the window, allowing the light panels to hang in their normal, softly pleated, resting position. Cassie left her room, descended the stairs and came upon Maxwell.

"Have you seen Romeo about?"

"No, my lady."

"Is he with Miss Lorna?"

"It would appear doubtful. From what I understand, Miss Lorna has gone driving with the Honorable Jeffrey Rutherford."

"Oh, I see." Which meant Mrs. Upton would be absent as well. "If you see Romeo you will let me know, won't you?"

"At once, my lady." Maxwell resumed his duties, leaving Cassie to locate the whereabouts of her terrier.

Cassie really didn't know where else to look. There was a remote chance that he could have gotten lost. However, Romeo preferred the company of people too much to run away. So that was one option she immediately ruled out. A squirrel could have distracted him and led him on a wild chase beyond the boundaries of the estate.

She clasped her hands behind her back and started for the back door. A low spine-tingling growl permeated the air. Chills ran up Cassie's arms and caused her to stop dead in her tracks.

It was Romeo's growl.

She followed the sound down the corridor, stopping just short at the library doors. As Cassie peered around the doorway, she saw clenched in Romeo's jaws some fabric or perhaps an article of clothing. Squire Stewart, the opponent, held the other end in a game of tug.

Romeo noticed his mistress' presence and released the linen clenched with desperation in his teeth. The suddenly free end threw the competitive squire off guard, sending him backward with his arms flying. Off balance, limbs flailing, he finally landed flat on his backside.

Cassie could not stop her laughter from escaping.

Still sitting on the floor, the squire pushed himself up with his arms. She could sense his reluctance to peer over his shoulder, afraid that someone might have seen his undignified antics.

"I am sorry"—Cassie stopped herself from chuckling as she spoke but her voice still wavered—"I didn't mean to disturb you."

The squire rose to his feet, brushed at his clothing and tugged at his cuffs, straightening his shirtsleeves. "My fault really," he replied. He flashed a warm smile at Romeo, who in turn showed his affection by wagging his tail. "If one plays rough, someone is bound to be hurt. Besides, it was all in good fun. Wasn't it, boy?" He bent and gave Romeo a good-natured pat on the head.

Clearly Romeo enjoyed his company. That spoke volumes for the squire's character. Perhaps Cassie had been too harsh at judging him and too quick to dismiss his offer to accompany her for a morning ride. The thought of spending any amount of time with him had been unbearable but now . . . now Cassie looked upon him the slightest bit more favorably.

Romeo dropped the knotted rag at the squire's feet and backed from it, as if daring him to take it.

Her pet seemed very fond of the man.

The squire snatched the toy and cried, "Aha! I've finally got it, you rascal." He then lobbed it across the room.

Romeo scrambled across the floor toward his prize. Cassie grew concerned that his claws might damage the expensive carpet with his rough play.

The squire seemed wholly unconcerned with the carpet, only delighting in Romeo's fun. Cassie thought she truly might reconsider the man's merits.

Romeo recaptured the toy and shook it while trapped between his teeth. He ran to Cassie and dropped it at her feet. It was her turn to toss for him.

"We should be doing this outside," Cassie said to the dog as much as to the man.

"Nonsense, in here is as good a place as any," said the squire. "We've plenty of open space."

Had he meant in front of the well-stocked bookshelves or the area in front of the hearth, around the two winged-back leather chairs?

Cassie used her forefinger and thumb to pick up the sodden, knotted rag and held it gingerly. "Very well, pet." Cassie meant the endearment for Romeo, not the squire, and tossed the toy across the room.

"Well done." The squire praised her.

"Sir," she directed at Squire Stewart.

"My lady?"

"I would like to accept your offer for a morning ride." Cassie managed a genuine, effortless smile. "If you have not changed your mind."

The squire regarded her then said, "It would be my pleasure. Shall we say at nine tomorrow morning?"

"I shall be waiting at the stables." She accepted with a slight incline of her head then had a sudden surge of remorse. "I thank you, sir. You are most gracious." But that was not precisely Cassie's true feelings.

Dinner that evening was a quiet affair. As always, Lorna dominated the conversation during the meal with her talk of men and parties.

Neither Lady Cassandra nor Julian spoke of the arrangement they'd made for the next morning. The few times their gazes met across the table, it surprised him to see a fleeting, temperate glance from her instead of the usual contempt-filled glare.

The knowledge that only the two of them knew of their plans felt delicious. Maxwell, who would never breathe a word to another, might have known. It was, after all, the butler who'd suggested the squire take this arduous step out of his sphere of comfort.

After everyone had finished eating, Julian excused himself and retreated to the library. The ladies bid him, "Good evening," and retired into their parlor.

All seemed calm and equitable. Life around Stewart Hall looked very well, indeed.

Dressed in her new bottle-green riding habit, Cassie arrived at the stables and found the squire waiting for her. He greeted her with more enthusiasm than before. Had she not known better, she might believe that he may actually be looking forward to their impending outing.

Their horses stood ready: A small chestnut with a sidesaddle and a light bay for the squire. Cassie approached the chestnut and stroked his neck. She stepped onto the mounting block and settled into the saddle.

Cassie moved her horse forward, away from the barn. The squire placed his foot into the iron and pushed off the ground to mount. He slipped and the boot in the iron dropped to the ground.

The bay shied, moving away from him. Cassie

could not watch after the second attempt. She presumed there might have been a third. Subsequently, squire, horse, and groom disappeared around the corner where Cassie had used the mounting block. The squire might have used it as well for he emerged atop his horse, ready to leave the grounds.

"It has been quite a while since I've ridden," he admitted to her, as more of a humble apology than excuse. "Although my brain may remember what to do, my limbs may not be up to the task."

"Then we shall not overtax you," Cassie offered. "May I suggest we keep today's excursion to a minimum?"

"A splendid idea. I thank you for your kind understanding and consideration." With an incline of his head he accepted her proposal. He led the way out of the stable area and onto the road. "Would it be permissible to have Romeo come along? I dare say he'd enjoy himself immensely."

"I don't think so. Father and I would leave Romeo behind when taking afternoon rides in the country, fearing he might be lost or trampled upon by the horses' hooves."

"Perhaps we could find a way to provide him with a saddle of his own or a perch of some sort."

How kind of the squire to consider her pet. Cassie had never thought him capable of any type of benevolent feelings. She'd been wrong.

"I think I am ready to post, but I should warn you

it may not last for long." He urged his mount into a trot and Cassie kept her horse next to his.

They rode into town and once around the park at a leisurely canter before returning to Stewart Hall.

They met in the breakfast room after their outing. Julian's legs felt more like jelly and he wasn't sure if descending the stairs would be his undoing. He might have landed in a heap on the ground floor. That would have been more embarrassing than the three attempts at mounting his horse that morning.

To his relief, Lady Cassandra had been the first to visit the sideboard and she was already seated by the time he arrived. Thank goodness. He did not know how he would have managed to rise when she entered the room. As it was, how he would manage to stand and leave in a half hour's time, he had no idea.

"I would like to thank you for this morning," she said to him. "It was nice to be out in the fresh air and I had forgotten how much I missed riding."

"Even with me as an escort? I am woefully under-skilled as an equestrian." He noticed she had added a plate of eggs to her usual solitary slice of toast.

"You are sure to improve, especially if we make it a daily habit." She glanced over the rim of her cup at him.

"It is my sincerest hope I can regain my strength by tomorrow so we might venture out again." Without feeling self–conscious, Julian felt encouraged at her words. "I would be quite ashamed to be held to

Edward's standards. He is accomplished at every endeavor he attempts."

Cassie could hear the pain and vulnerability in his voice. She couldn't imagine what caused him to continue.

"I've never been good on my feet. It's not a well known fact," he went on to say, "but I don't know how to dance." He didn't seem to express any shame. "Right now I suppose I do harbor some regrets." His soft, kind hazel eyes met Cassie's. "I know Lorna wanted her first waltz to be with Edward. I'm afraid I will not be able to accommodate her."

Was he truly admitting his weakness to her? "I could instruct you," she offered and then wondered why she'd said those words. She could read the uncertainty in his eyes. "For Lorna's sake. I believe there is more than enough time for you to learn, to perfect the steps, if you are willing."

The squire remained quiet.

Cassie did not know what to think. Was he angry? Embarrassed at his situation? Of his confession? Or perhaps that she knew of it at all?

Taking advantage of the silence, she left her seat and moved to his side, holding her hand out to him. He stood, although hesitantly, almost as if his legs would not propel him forward.

"Here, let me show you the basic step." She took him by the arm and drew him to a corner that permitted movement.

Lifting her skirt to allow her feet to be seen, she stood across from him. Slowly, she talked him through the steps.

"On the first beat, you step out here." He followed. "On the second, you bring your other foot near. And on the third beat, shift your weight back on the first foot." The squire continued to follow her lead. "It isn't difficult in the least."

"One, two, three . . . one, two, three . . . one, two, three . . ." he said just above a whisper and mirrored her feet.

"It's best not to count aloud." Cassie smiled. "There . . . I think you've got it."

She gazed up into his face. He was smiling too. He was smiling *at* her. Cassie felt quite self-conscious at his extended gaze and quickly averted her eyes.

"Of course, this is not the correct position to dance." She was quick to clarify.

"Yes, I am well aware of that aspect," he added softly and cleared his throat. "I have *seen* the waltz performed many times."

The squire took Cassie's right hand in his left. She brushed against the smooth metal of his signet ring. He moved closer and slipped his other hand around her waist. All hint of expression fell from his face. A long bout of silence followed. She swallowed hard.

Squire Stewart held her in his arms, dance position. With a brave upward tilt of her chin, she slowly turned her head, displaying a cool, seemingly detached profile.

In reality, Cassie felt the panic rise through her. Her pulse raced and she could feel her heart pound hard. She wondered if he could hear it too. Her first reaction was to flee but she managed to keep her head.

"There doesn't seem to be enough room in here to turn." Moving away from him, she nervously smiled. "Perhaps this is enough for today. Shall we continue tomorrow?"

He met his instructor's eyes and nodded. "If it is not too much of an inconvenience."

"Until tomorrow then." Cassie inclined her head and took her leave. She moved down the hall and slipped into a side parlor, closing the solid door behind her. Leaning her head onto the cool surface, she inhaled slowly to calm her wildly beating heart.

What was happening to her? What was this feeling bubbling up inside her? While the squire held her close, she thought she felt as if she would faint. She wanted to be as far away from him as possible.

Cassie vividly recalled the warmth of his hand and his firm grip on her waist. It was horrifying and comforting all at the same time and she wondered why she had not felt this way when Edward took her in his arms.

Chapter Seven

Julian looked forward to every morning when he could spend time alone with Lady Cassandra. After their ride, he sat across the breakfast table for coffee. Some evenings, he escorted her to various parties in Edward's absence. When working at home, he often walked by the side parlor, where the women sat after supper, to see her in animated conversation with Lorna or enjoying a book by the fireside.

This afternoon Mrs. Green wheeled the clattering tea cart into the library. Julian redirected her to the front parlor, thinking the brightly lit room conducive to a more enjoyable afternoon tea.

He pulled on his jacket before venturing out of the house to call the ladies in. The squire imagined that Lady Cassandra had lost all sense of time. He knew he could find her with Romeo, with or without Lorna depending on his sister's social schedule, far beyond in the rear gardens.

During the precious few minutes it took Julian to walk the path from the manor to the lawn, he shortened his stride and slowed his pace to delay his arrival. Although Romeo would always be the first to notice his unannounced approach, his presence would soon be detected by the ladies as well.

The squire allowed himself to witness the expression of delight on their faces when they first spotted him. He found himself envying Edward. With all the talents and advantages his younger brother had, it was the first and only time Julian ever remembered feeling this way.

However, his life would not be at all bad. He and Lady Cassandra would be in-laws and that would ensure their continual contact through the years. He could share in her pleasant company and he felt that would be sufficient.

Julian took his time walking to the clearing beyond the topiary, feeling the soft crunch of gravel beneath his feet. The sound itself was soothing and strangely satisfying. Once he was spotted, Romeo would wag his tail and the ladies would wave to greet him.

Romeo barked, sounding the alarm at his approach. Julian waved, only . . . Lorna was not there. Lady Cassandra returned his wave. She and Romeo headed in the squire's direction.

"This is becoming quite a habit." A smile graced his normally staid face.

"I suppose it is, isn't it?" Lady Cassandra's beaming face made him wish he could prolong this moment together. "Shall we have tea in the library?"

"No, I thought it too nice to pass up this delightful afternoon. The view of the front gardens is quite breathtaking from the front parlor."

With a nod, she turned to start for the house.

"I shall ask your indulgence before we go in for tea, if I may."

She turned back to face the squire.

"There is plenty of room out here." He gestured holding his arms open wide. "Shall we take a moment and continue my waltz instruction?"

Cassie looked around. "This is a most unorthodox place to dance." She looked back at him and narrowed her eyes. "I suppose it will suffice."

"Lorna's first waltz at Almack's is only a few days away. I do not want to disappoint her."

Cassie believed that. She had seen both brothers display devotion for their sister. And there was probably nothing he would not do to please her.

"Here Romeo!" Lady Cassandra called. The terrier bounded to her. "Sit right there. Stay!" Romeo promptly obeyed.

The squire stepped closer and took his position in front of Cassie. She looked into his lean, handsome face.

Handsome? Exactly when did she think of his face as being handsome?

"Lady Cassandra? Are you ready to begin?"

Cassie could feel the warmth of his hand on her back. Her hand in his, held motionless. Now acutely aware that only inches separated his body from hers, she thought it best to start instead of dwelling on him.

"The music will begin." Cassie begun to hum a non-descript tune in three-quarters time. Her head dipped in deliberate motion with every passing beat.

The squire's mouth formed the count of the beat. *One, two, three . . . one, two, three . . . one, two, three . . .* Growing accustomed to her tune, he began to step side to side with the music.

"You are not supposed to move your mouth," she reminded him, and what a nice-looking mouth it was. It could form the kindest, most tender smile.

Cassie had to admit, he was *very* handsome. His high cheekbones led to the gentle arch of his dark brow. Following the line of his face, his jaw squared off at his chin. There she detected a slight dimple. She hadn't noticed that before nor had she ever been this close to him for such an extended period of time.

Romeo stayed where he was told. His head, however, dipped and turned, following the couple as he continued to watch their dance progress.

The squire took a step, Cassie followed his lead. He turned her slowly in time to the a cappella music, then another turn and another. Each turn became tighter and faster than the one before, spinning round and round until the squire's toe caught a tuft of unevenly growing grass. He stumbled, plunging toward the ground, bringing Cassie down with him.

Cassie let out a cry, then grunted when she hit the ground.

"I do beg your pardon!" Squire Stewart landed on his left hand, sparing his partner from taking his crushing weight. "Are you quite all right?"

Romeo bounded toward the collapsed bodies barking with concern.

"I do beg your pardon!" the squire repeated. "Have you been injured?"

Romeo leaped at Cassie trying to lick her face, as if it would help. The pet then leaped at the squire and sniffed at him as well, checking his well-being.

Sitting up, Cassie found herself stunned but unharmed. Looking at the squire's disheveled hair and grass-stained cuff, not to mention his cravat which sat askew, she broke into unrestrained laughter.

"Lady Cassandra?" the squire sounded concerned. He must have thought she had bumped her head in the fall or perhaps was having a hysterical reaction.

Her laughing continued.

"I'm afraid I'm quite the clumsy clod," he uttered, trying to take the entire blame. "I just hope that it's not contagious."

"It serves us right for dancing in such an inappropriate place."

The squire took another look around and must have noticed as she had that the footing was poor. They were lucky that one of them did not twist an ankle or break a leg.

"You are right of course." She certainly would not have placed the blame on him.

He stood and finished brushing off his pantaloons then reached out his hand to help her up off the ground. "Are you sure you are not hurt?" He watched her move, looking for a twinge of pain.

"You *are* a mother hen!" Cassie brushed herself off. "Let's go in for tea, shall we?" The squire watched her head for the house, her grass-stained skirts swaying side to side. "Come, Romeo!"

Lorna insisted that Lady Cassandra join them at the Stoddards' ball that night. Julian did not express an opinion and left the decision entirely to the ladies.

The three of them rode in the coach. Julian dared not look at Lady Cassandra to avoid any speculation on his sister's part that something other than civility might be going on between them. It would be like her to misinterpret and exaggerate the tentative association he and Lady Cassandra had managed.

Once they'd arrived at Lord and Lady Stoddard's, Lorna entered the room followed by Lady Cassandra. Julian's breath caught. Lovely Lady Cassandra in an azure-blue gown. The drop shoulder sleeves gave the gown a dramatic line. The low décolletage might have been too daring without an added sheer mull. The material was softly gathered at the neck by a ribbon that enchantingly trailed down her back.

Julian ran his fingers over the folds in his not-so-intricately tied cravat and tugged down on his burgundy waistcoat. All of a sudden he felt self-conscious and wholly inadequate standing next to her. He noticed the small fragrant rosebuds she wore in a headband, lending a delicate scent to her hair.

Julian had the good fortune to meet up with his friend and occasional business associate Sir Horace Boyer. He managed to beg him for a dance—not for himself, mind, but for a Lady Cassandra. Once setting his eyes upon the lady, Horace was not bothered in the least to do his friend a favor. Julian made the introductions and Horace led Lady Cassandra away.

During the dainty measures of the dance, the squire noticed Lord Nathan Ellerby paying particular attention to the couple. Ellerby, the third son of an earl, was a friend of Edward's. Edward had frequently referred to his friend as 'Nefarious Nathan.'

Ellerby crossed the room and oiled his way to Sir Horace after he had left the dance floor. "Good evening to you, sir," Ellerby said, making his presence known to Horace.

"Lord Ellerby . . ." Horace turned to face him.

"May I impose upon you for an introduction"—Ellerby hadn't waited for Horace to respond and continued—"to that lovely creature in blue you've abandoned on the other side of the room."

Horace looked at his recent dance partner in her azure gown. "Ah . . . that would be the Lady Cassandra Phillips."

Even from where he stood, Julian caught a gleam in Ellerby's dark eyes suggesting he had an ulterior motive.

"I suppose it couldn't do any harm . . ." Sir Horace flustered. Somehow the significance of an introduction escaped him. Julian had wanted to stop him—shout across the room if need be—but his good manners prevented him.

Ellerby's well-known reputation as a ladies' man only exceeded Edward's, and Julian wondered what Nefarious Nathan could possibly want with Lady Cassandra.

"Ah, Lady Cassandra . . . may I, may I present, ah . . . Lord Nathan Ellerby."

Lord Nathan performed a grand sweeping bow.

"How do you do," Cassie replied.

In rising, he stepped toward her, taking her hand. "Lady Cassandra, the pleasure is all mine, I assure you."

Not wasting another moment, he ushered her to one side, away from Sir Horace. A string of exorbitant compliments sprang superfluously from the newly introduced gentleman.

"You waste your words on me, sir." Quick to put him in his place, she added, "I am engaged to Mr. Edward Stewart."

"Tender to beauty is never wasted." Lord Nathan placed a light kiss on the back of her hand. "I can appreciate your company as well as Mr. Stewart."

She could feel her cheek warm at the thought that he might appreciate her company.

"Would you care to share the next set?" Lord Ellerby seemed to sense her trepidation and continued. "I loathe to allow such loveliness to sit by the wayside. It would be such a shame for you not to enjoy yourself because of your betrothed's absence." His well-practiced smile showed a row of perfectly shaped white teeth, much like that of a shark.

Cassie looked for the squire. Perhaps he would come to her aid. But she could not see him in the crowd. Finding it impossible to refuse Lord Nathan's request, she agreed. A minute later he took her to the floor for a waltz.

Julian managed to make it across the room to Horace but not before he'd made the introductions and far too late to stop Ellerby from escorting Lady Cassandra to the dance floor.

Julian watched the villain gather Lady Cassandra into his arms. A protective feeling began to grow. He felt certain Edward would never allow such an event to take place. However, she was not the squire's intended therefore he felt it was not his place to object.

"Horace?" The squire, feeling both displeasure and a need for an expeditious explanation, clapped his friend on the shoulder, preventing him from moving forward. "Whatever possessed you to introduce that devil to Lady Cassandra?"

"I didn't think there was any harm, really." Horace shrugged. "He was rather insistent, you know, Julian."

"As I can well imagine." How well he knew Ellerby's persuasive nature. The squire didn't like associating with him in business and certainly didn't want to deal with him on a personal level. "Do me a favor, will you?"

"Another? All you need do is ask. You know that."

"Escort Lady Cassandra away as soon as she returns. I don't want her to be exposed to Ellerby any longer than need be."

"Don't blame you at all. I shall be more than happy to oblige."

Lady Cassandra and Ellerby twirled amongst the crowd. Horace's gaze stayed fixed upon them. After the dance ended, Julian watched her and nodded to his friend to make his move. After this next set the squire would see that he and Lady Cassandra made their exit, leaving Nefarious Nathan behind.

The next morning, Maxwell stared out the front window, watching a transport race down the road toward Stewart Hall. Moments after the hansom rolled to a stop, the door flew open. Sir Horace Boyer took a passing glance at his surroundings before disembarking and stepping toward the front door.

Maxwell pulled the door open directly. Sir Horace stepped inside handing over his hat, cane, and gloves.

"Where's Julian? I must speak to him at once!" Sir Horace's voice held an unmistakable sense of urgency.

"The squire is in the library, sir." Maxwell draped the guest's coat over his arm and took hold of the hat and cane.

"I'll announce myself." Sir Horace walked toward the library with weighted purpose. Boldly stepping through the open door, he came to an abrupt halt when he spotted Squire Stewart.

Julian sat comfortably with his fingers steepled, next to the large paned window that overlooked the side garden. His eyes stared aimlessly out into the box-hedged garden. He heard a light knock on the door.

"Horace, how good it is to see you! Come in! Come in!" Even though his friend had caused some trouble by introducing Lady Cassandra to Ellerby, he had also allowed them to escape without alarm.

Horace stepped into the library and moved toward the window as if he wanted to see what Julian was watching.

"What, may I ask, is the reason for this unexpected pleasure?" Julian shook Horace's hand and motioned for his guest to take the seat opposite his desk. "Another potential profitable business opportunity, perhaps?" Julian noticed Horace's grim response. If he were here on business, the news would not be pleasant.

By his manner, it must have been grave, very grave indeed.

Horace sunk into the chair very slowly and spoke in a low, serious voice. "You'd best have a seat as well."

"Why Horace, I don't believe I've ever seen you in such a state. Good Gad, Horace, what is it?"

"Very bad news I fear." He sighed. Horace obviously didn't know where to begin. "News of the *King's Quest* has just arrived. It departed the continent two days ago for Dover. She's been reported missing."

"Missing? The *King's Quest*?" Julian's voice sounded hollow. He stared into the center of the room, focusing on nothing in particular, just staring, feeling numb. "It isn't possible. There must be some sort of mistake." Julian looked back at Horace. "Edward is scheduled to return on that ship."

"I know. That's why I've come. I didn't want you to read it in the *Gazette*."

Could it be that Edward was . . . Julian rubbed his throbbing forehead. His mind tried to put all the pieces together. He tried to fathom the thought of never seeing his brother again.

"They've already sent several rescue ships. They

reported finding only debris. No survivors, no bodies recovered. Not yet." Horace watched Julian for a reaction. "Shall I get you a brandy?"

"No." Julian turned toward his guest. "I must tell Lorna, she'll be quite upset. She and Edward have always been very close."

"And Lady Cassandra," Horace added. "He is, after all . . . they were to be wed."

"Yes, and Lady Cassandra." How would she take this news? It would certainly be better if she heard this from him rather than a stranger or through the rumor mill.

Horace followed the squire out of the house. They found the ladies in the back garden. Lorna and Cassie were busy playing with Romeo on the grassy area. The ladies tossed the ball between them and laughed with delight.

When Romeo abandoned his game to greet the squire properly, the ladies noticed the gentlemen approaching and headed toward them. Cassie glanced at Lorna who apparently also sensed the grim climate.

"What is it? What's happened?" Lorna spoke first. The men exchanged staid glances. "Julian?"

"I think we should all go inside and sit down," the squire suggested. Lorna nodded and began to walk slowly to the house with Sir Horace.

"No, I want to know now." Cassie stood her ground and refused to move until she got her answer.

Lorna and Sir Horace continued, increasing their lead.

"What has happened?" Cassie demanded to know.

After nearly a minute of silence, he blurted out, "I'm afraid Edward is dead."

Chapter Eight

"What?" Cassandra gasped. The color drained from her face. Julian thought she might faint dead away.

He felt like a gudgeon for blurting out the news. Subtlety had never been one of his strengths. This would have been a perfect opportunity to have exercised any that he might have possessed.

"Well, perhaps not dead, but certainly presumed dead. Horace can give us further details once we are inside."

Without a word, she nodded. The squire offered his arm and she took it. Silence surrounded them and in no time they were entering through the back door. Romeo dashed ahead into the house.

"Lorna is waiting with Mrs. Upton in the parlor,"

Horace told Julian in the hallway. Julian acknowledged with a curt nod before the three of them entered.

Lorna took one look at Cassie and gasped, clearly frightened. "Cassie! Cassie? What's happened? Julian?" She clasped Mrs. Upton's hands and held tight as if she were still a small child.

Cassandra said nothing and made no action to indicate she had heard what anyone had said.

"Lorna," Julian began and took hold of her free hand. "I want to assure you that we will do everything we can, utilize every resource possible to ensure we are successful."

"With what?" She stared at her brother wide-eyed and confused. "What are you talking about?"

"The ship . . . your brother Edward—" Horace sounded equally as tactful as Julian. "I'm afraid it is lost at sea."

"What?" Lorna cried, her eyes filled with tears.

"This cannot be." Mrs. Upton pressed her handkerchief to her nose.

"His ship has gone missing," Horace stated directly.

"Does this mean he's . . . is he . . . d-dead?" Lorna forced the words out.

"No!" Julian nearly shouted. "As I said, we will employ every means available to find him. He is . . . missing. We *will* find him."

"Yes, yes, we'll find him." Lorna nodded and swiped away her tears.

"He's just missing. He'll be fine when we find him," Mrs. Upton repeated, seemingly to calm herself and Lorna.

"Perhaps you should go to your room and lie down for a bit," Horace suggested.

"That is an excellent idea for both the ladies," Julian replied. "Maxwell, send for Lady Cassandra's maid, would you?"

Maxwell, who seemed to have appeared out of the woodwork, acknowledged and stepped away.

"Mrs. Upton, please see Lorna to her room," the squire ordered. He helped Lorna to her feet and her governess took her by the arm.

Julian and Horace flanked Cassandra, helped her stand and walked her to the door. Moving into the great hall, Lavette met the advancing trio.

"*Ma pauvre petite.*" Lavette sighed at the first look of her mistress. She led Cassandra up the stairs and away to her room.

Horace followed the squire into the library. Moving to his desk, Julian began searching through his drawers. He retrieved a document which had an unmistakable legal appearance to it.

"Gad! That's not Edward's will is it?"

"Do you think me totally heartless? This is the will of the late Earl of Thadburry, Lady Cassandra's father. The earl has set up certain terms for her inheritance. I'm looking for the new clause since it appears that the circumstances have altered." He sat behind his desk and put on his spectacles to review the document. "Besides, I doubt Edward ever bothered to have a will drawn up."

"But you just said you were going to find him." Horace pointed toward the parlor where they sat and broke the news just moments ago.

"I know what I said and we will try to find him. But Lady Cassandra does not have the luxury of waiting. If it turns out Edward is . . . we will all deal with that when the time comes. For now, we don't know his fate, do we?"

Horace busied himself by pouring two glasses of sherry and setting one for the squire on the desk.

"Drink up, Julian, you need it." Horace motioned with his own glass. "You've had quite a shock. Trust me, it'll do you good."

The squire took the glass and peered over the top of his glasses at his friend.

Horace finished his sherry in a single swallow.

Julian took a sip and set the remainder aside. Horace refilled his glass and took a seat next to the squire.

After several minutes of paging through the document and rereading potentially pertinent clauses, he laid the paper down and pulled off his spectacles. Reaching for his sherry, Julian took another sip. What he had to do, what he had to inform Lady Cassandra she must do . . .

No, he was not looking forward to such a callous,

unfeeling maneuver, but it had to be done. With a final swallow, Julian drained his glass.

Life continued at Stewart Hall, accompanied by a gloomy veneer. Julian had hired his own men to investigate his brother's possible whereabouts but there was still no further news of Edward by the end of the week.

The squire feared that although his brother was not dead, only missing at this point, it would be impossible for Lady Cassandra to fulfill the terms of her father's will. It was far too soon to consider a memorial service and proclaim Edward dead, but would it be too late for her to comply with the clause enacted by his absence?

To give her every chance of retaining her inheritance, Julian had to be the bearer of additional bad news. He realized she would have no time for mourning, no time for acceptance, no time at all.

Here he stood, his arm stretched over the mantle. He turned his gaze from the flames on the log that held no answers.

Lady Cassandra's hands were neatly folded on her lap. Her perfectly oval face tilted in his direction. Her eyes focused on him, waiting for him to speak.

Julian did not know how he was going to tell her. Again, he felt his inadequacy to relay her father's request with the tact he thought necessary. However, with no alternative, he had to continue best he could.

"You must marry before your upcoming birthday," he said.

Cassandra burst into tears and covered her face.

Julian knew she would be upset. She must have been more in love with Edward than he thought.

He wanted to comfort her. Inappropriate perhaps, but he could not sit by and watch the effect of his brother's absence—the man she must have cared for a great deal—and how she must marry another, take its toll on her.

Julian reached out, his hand hovering barely an inch from her quivering shoulder. He turned her shoulder toward him. She let her head fall against his chest. A heartbeat later, his arms enveloped her into a comforting embrace. His platonic feeling soon gave way to something entirely new.

Cassandra's tear-stained face turned up at him. With her eyes open wide, she looked deeply into his. Julian leaned back, releasing his hold while he still had control.

"Please, sir, I am well." Her stare was momentarily interrupted by her dark lashes as she blinked.

The squire pulled a silk kerchief from his breast pocket and offered it from the palm of his hand. "I am sorry for you," he whispered in an unfamiliar, tender tone. "But it is stated in your father's will."

"I don't see how you can ask such a thing of me." Cassandra lifted the silk kerchief from his hand and allowed it to tumble open, cascading to its full length. She sniffed and blotted the moisture from her eyes.

Julian could not pull his gaze from her, no matter how hard he tried. "Your father's will states that since marriage to Edward is impossible that you must marry before you reach the age of twenty."

"That is only three weeks away! I can't possibly . . . how am I to find a husband . . . it is impossible!"

"I'm certain you can easily find another suitor." He felt odd and immediately regretted the words as they escaped from his lips.

"That is scandalous!" she gasped. "I should be in mourning."

"But he is not, has not been proclaimed dead." The squire regarded her. "This is the first I've seen you shed a tear over Edward. Even as you received the news you never cried."

"These are not tears for Edward," she whispered. "I'm very truly sorry to hear of your brother's fate. I do not wish him ill but I do not regard his absence as a personal loss on my part."

"I thought you were in love with him." Julian hesitated for the briefest moment. He'd never even considered that. "Is there someone else you care for?"

"I admit, I was never in love with Edward. He is—was—a fine man; thoughtful, kind, perhaps I thought him too immature and compulsive for my taste.

However, if I admit my affection for another, you may think me forward."

"No, please. I believe this is the time to be honest. If there is . . . someone you wish to . . . well, you must marry and if you can find true happiness . . ."

"Very well." Cassandra glanced away and took a deep breath, gathering courage. "It's true. I do have feelings for another. He is a widower, a little older than I."

Again, her beautiful eyes lifted to meet his.

A spark of hope sprang into Julian's heart. Was it not morbid to be glad of his brother's absence, perhaps his demise, and wish his bride for himself? Did he have a chance with this lovely angel? For her to reveal feelings for him was more than he could hope for. Pure fantasy.

And yet . . . Julian felt his insides melt at her gaze—the deep liquid pools of her dark blue eyes. He was lost. He gasped for air, only to realize that his mouth was upon hers in a tender kiss.

"No!" The squire moved away from her and shook his head. "I cannot allow this to happen. This is not acceptable!"

"By that kiss, I gather that you harbor the same feelings for me, or am I mistaken?"

"Well . . . I . . . no! It is inappropriate!" Bewildered by his action, he wondered how his control had managed to slip. It was not like him.

Gaining some distance, his head began to clear

and his priorities returned. His blood began to cool, he regained his composure and he felt ready to recite his arguments. "I am the executor of your father's will. I am legally and morally bound to make sure his wishes are carried out. I cannot—"

"Did that kiss mean nothing?" Her eyes still burned with the intensity he had felt in her lips.

"It was something that should not have happened. It was a mistake, clear and simple." He straightened, smoothed his hair and adjusted his waistcoat.

"We shall see, sir." Cassie would make him take back every word.

That kiss was much, much more than the meeting of lips. Only moments before, her heart had pounded fiercely in her chest, then came to a stop as he neared. In his eyes, she saw the same passion and longing that was inside of her.

She felt the warmth of his breath upon her cheek. He was going to kiss her and she very much wanted him to. Her lips ached in anticipation.

Then he pulled her toward him, causing her to abandon any thought as to what was proper, and kissed her. She knew with each short, stolen breath that she loved him.

Certain as she was about her feelings, Cassie knew he must share them. She had sensed the desire and the passion in those few fleeting moments. He could try to deny it but that would have been a lie.

"You will dress in your most attractive gown and I

shall escort you to Almack's tomorrow night myself. You *will* begin circulating. If you wish to keep Hedgeway Park you will need to find a husband." His voice regained its normal authoritative bearing, ordering her about again. "Furthermore, you will remove that mourning gown for a more suitable dress, is that understood?"

"I supposed this old frock could not attract any gentleman." It hadn't deterred him one bit. "I will do as you ask and dress as alluring and enchanting as I can manage." If he wanted her to lure a husband, she would oblige him. "I suppose *any* man will do?"

Silence momentarily encompassed them as he considered her words. "I would hope that you might find him agreeable. I would not wish you to wed a monster."

She curtsied, inclining her head only slightly in submission. "As you wish, Squire." It was only then a plan began to form.

Later that evening, Cassie entered the drawing room and eased into her favorite, comfortable, overstuffed chair with a novel. She opened the book to the page where she had left off. Her eyes scanned over the words without comprehension. She stared blankly at the page while her mind reflected to that afternoon with the squire in his study and that unforgettable kiss.

Romeo sprang onto the chair and into Cassie's lap.

She patted him welcome with a smile and Lorna swept into the room.

"Julian told me you were teaching him how to waltz so he won't look like a simpleton at Almack's."

"He told you?" Cassie found herself shocked that the squire would admit to his younger sister his shortcoming and his indebtedness to another, especially a woman.

"I thought it might help if you had music to practice." She held out an ornately decorated box.

"I don't really think this is a good time," Cassie replied. The squire had spent most of that day in the library, clearly avoiding her.

"Edward brought this back from Austria last year." Lorna sounded a bit sad at the mention of her brother. She glanced at the precious possession and ran her hand over the smooth lid. "I'm sure he'll have something just as exceptional when he finally returns from this trip." She brightened, obviously hoping for the best outcome.

Cassie took the music box. A closer look revealed an intricate, inlaid pattern of different colored woods adorning the delicate instrument.

"Edward *is* coming back. I just know he is, but he won't be here in time for the dance tomorrow. So I do wish Julian could dance with me," Lorna sighed. "For both our sakes, we would be spared the humiliation."

The top felt smooth and Cassie lifted the lid. A delicate tune to a three-quarters time emerged.

"Thank you, Lorna. I believe it will be of great help." Cassie had no intention of putting it to use at the moment.

"I'll go and tell Julian right away!" Lorna responded with delight in the knowledge that she had in some small way helped her brother overcome his social inadequacy. She spun away from the drawing room to speak to him.

Several minutes later, Lorna returned, dragging the squire behind her. She was more than excited for him to proceed with his instruction.

"Shall we adjourn to the ballroom?" Lorna suggested.

"If that is what you wish," the squire agreed, eager to please his sister.

"I'll have the ballroom lit right away!" Lorna dashed off again.

"Only the corner, mind you!" he called after her in hopes of curbing his over-enthusiastic sibling.

Cassie sat quietly, waiting for the squire to be the first to speak.

"After you, my lady." He swept his hand toward the door.

"Since I have no idea where we are headed"— Cassie mimicked his gesture—"after you, sir."

He gave her a stern look as if he knew she was being purposely difficult and proceeded down the hallway.

Entering the ballroom, Julian was satisfied to see

that less than half the ballroom had been lit as he had requested. He dreaded the notion of being alone with Cassandra. To hold her in his arms might be more than he could bear.

The grand room was expansive and the lack of lighting concealed the far end in darkness. Chairs lined the plainly decorated walls on both sides. The colorful guests were meant to supply the room's ornamentation, but it had been a very long time since this room had seen any type of merriment.

Julian held the music box in his hands. In a bittersweet memory, he recalled when Edward had presented the gift to Lorna. She was in awe of its beauty and foreign origin. He lifted the lid and a lilting tune rose from the box. The squire hesitantly turned to his instructor.

"Shall we begin?" Cassandra's eyes sparkled in the dim light. She stepped closer to him and held out her arms. The smile on her face, so lovely. Her open arms, so hard to resist.

"I would not wish to disappoint Lorna," he said aloud for his benefit as well as Cassandra's. He stepped closer.

"Of course not. She expects you to lead her in her first waltz."

Julian wiped his damp palms against his trousers before taking Cassandra into his arms and beginning to dance.

The dim light of the room added a dreamlike

quality to the atmosphere. He turned her slowly and moved around the edge of the room. It was no wonder the waltz was considered an immoral dance. Even someone such as he, who thought himself to be immune to the influence of a woman, could feel the effect.

Switching direction, Julian began to feel almost dizzy. Other men who did not have the control he had would certainly succumb to the temptation. No wonder his brother had such a weakness for women. He could see that if one spent a great deal of time in a woman's company, one could easily become victim to a certain lady's charms.

Concentration on the dance steps and a conscious effort not to step on his partner's toes kept his mind working. He suspected if he allowed his mind a moment to stray, his desires would carry him off.

The feel of her in his arms, her fragrance drifting up from her soft hair and creamy skin, became more and more intoxicating with every revolution.

They continued to dance flawlessly and they kept in time to the slowing music. As the tune became a background of unrecognizable notes, he and Cassandra stood in each other's arms staring at one another. Truth be known, his willpower was weakening.

Would he be able to dance with her tomorrow night and not appear an absolute flat? Would he embarrass himself by gazing adoringly at her as if he were a love-struck lad?

Chapter Nine

The dreaded evening finally arrived. The squire waited for Cassandra on the landing, surveying the guests of Almack's. Relieved of her pelisse, she approached him. He was unable to tear his gaze from her golden sarcenet dress. The unadorned low décolletage displayed her shoulders and more cleavage than she had dared before. And was his mind playing tricks on him or was the dress translucent?

It was not his place to voice an opinion. His warming feelings for her were irrelevant—nor did he have the time to delve into exactly what they were. He had a duty to perform and that was to see to the late earl's wishes.

"Does this meet with your approval?" Cassandra smiled in triumph at her obvious impact on him and batted her dark lashes for further dramatics. "Might you believe I can catch the notice of any gentlemen tonight?"

The squire cleared the obstruction from his throat and managed a reply. "Yes, quite nice." He leaned closer and whispered, "You should not waste the opportunity. There are many eligible men here and more than one suitable. I must encourage you to make an effort." He could see turbulence brewing in her eyes.

"You may be quite assured, sir, I shall."

He escorted her to join the assembly. Clearly Cassandra was not pleased with what she had to do but she would do it.

She displayed a warm glowing smile toward the gathering, welcoming whatever and whoever might come her way. Julian was pleased to have Horace partner her for a first dance.

The squire stood to one side of the crowded room and watched. Next to him stood an exclusive male trio, their eyes transfixed on Cassandra moving across the floor.

"Say Jared, isn't that Edward Stewart's intended?" Daniel Thompson asked, the eldest of the three.

"I believe *was* is a more appropriate description," Colin Henderson remarked.

"What are you saying, Henderson?" Thompson quipped.

"I believe poor Edward met with an untimely

demise. It's said he was aboard the *King's Quest* when it sank a while back."

Thompson reached up to his throat to straighten his already perfectly tied cravat. "Poor sot."

"Poor girl, you mean," Jared Gilbert sighed. "Stewart was quite the cad, you know. She deserves better than his like." Gilbert smoothed any unsightly creases on his waistcoat.

"Agreed," Thompson spouted. "However, I wouldn't want to subject myself to a potentially scandalous situation and court her myself." The other two nodded, all in complete agreement.

Julian noticed Lord Nathan Ellerby standing on the other side of the young men, listening to every word. He did not wait to make his move toward Cassandra before the young men dispersed.

"Well, best be off," Gilbert announced.

"Quite right, Jared." Thompson eyed his two companions.

"The ladies are waiting." Henderson looked across the room, planning his route perhaps?

"'Tis time to do the pretty." Gilbert gave the cuffs of his shirt a final tug.

The three men parted, disappearing into the crowd.

The squire watched the young trio with interest and caught Ellerby making his calculated approach. With position, wealth and a title, Ellerby should prove to be more than a suitable match for Lady Cassandra—

if she should snare the confirmed bachelor. Did it really matter that the squire didn't personally care for him?

Julian remembered the first ball Cassandra attended at the Addisons'. Ellerby had been quite disappointed to hear Cassandra was betrothed to Edward. Tonight Ellerby had no obstacles to overcome. Julian neared the couple to listen.

". . . *and* a waltz?" Cassandra's voice rang out in laughter. "Lord Nathan, that would raise a few eyebrows, would it not?"

"Do not let that worry you. I, for one, intend to have a marvelous time." His dark eyes gazed up at her with a devilish twinkle.

"I grant you your wish, sir." She smiled.

He straightened. "Then I look forward to our *first* dance together." Off to Ellerby's left, the squire noticed the onslaught of Gilbert, Henderson, and Thompson.

"I best be off and let the lads try to impress you." With a small respectful nod, he disappeared.

Seconds later in Ellerby's place stood three young men, vying for Cassandra's attention. To their delight, she accommodated them all by promising each a dance.

As the strings tuned, Julian made his way to Cassandra's side to remind her of their dance. He had hoped a prominent display on the dance floor would encourage interest. He knew now the exhibition would be unnecessary. Lady Cassandra was a social success and would not have any problem attracting gentlemen.

Throughout the evening Cassie laughed, smiled and chatted with the various men who came to pay their respects and to those lucky enough to dance with her. Glancing over the shoulders of her potential suitors, or out of the corner of her eye, she made certain Squire Stewart observed her every move. She was pleased the gentlemen found her amiable but she did not enjoy it half as much as she led the squire to believe.

His normally granite facade showed minute signs of agitation. He must have convinced himself to keep his personal sentiments to himself. Cassie was equally determined to do all she could to see that he failed.

Julian truly believed persuading Cassie to marry was for her own good. He, however, did not feel it a wise choice to stand on the side and watch. The squire could not stop the knot tightening in his stomach every time she took to the floor on the arm of another man. Nor the pounding in his head that threatened to make him scream when she bestowed one of her delightful smiles upon another.

Julian half-heartedly led Lorna around the dance floor in her first waltz. Instead of attending to his partner, he turned and twisted his head to keep a watch on Cassandra.

"Do pay attention, Julian," Lorna scolded him.

"I am sorry." He reluctantly allowed Cassandra to slip from sight and faced his sister. He continued to steal glimpses across the dance floor at Ellerby and Cassandra.

When the dance ended, Ellerby displayed his most gracious manners and escorted Cassandra back to the squire. It was all done very proper, but this cur's false propriety did not fool Julian.

"I would like to ask permission to call on you to-morrow afternoon," Ellerby asked. "Perhaps I might take you for a drive through the park?"

"Well . . ." Cassandra eyed the squire's expression and she must have guessed his general growing displeasure. Her attention returned to Ellerby. "I think I'd enjoy that, thank you."

"Good, I think it best if we keep our outings discreet." He made it sound as if he were making a grand chivalrous gesture. "I would not want to cause any unnecessary talk. I recognize the delicate situation at present."

"I appreciate your discretion. I'm not so sure any-one else would be as courageous as you to tempt a possible scandal by calling on me so soon after my . . . Mr. Stewart's . . . absence."

"*Scandal?* If you only knew what that man . . ." Julian grumbled under his breath.

After Lord Nathan left, Cassie decided he was the perfect antagonist for the squire. As to Lord Nathan, his lordship would certainly not allow his heart to become involved with her, of that she felt quite certain. She smiled in satisfaction. Yes, Lord Nathan would do very nicely.

Lady Cassandra and Lorna talked and laughed all the way home, much to the displeasure of the squire who had to relive the women's triumphs—the gossip, the dancing, and the gentlemen.

Upon reaching Stewart Hall, Julian retired to the solitude of the library. The familiar leather-bound books that filled the walls welcomed him. He ran his hand over the front edge of the heavy desk.

It had been his father's, still as solid as the day it had been made. It afforded a comfort along with the countless number of objects that had lined the shelves ever since he could remember, but this night they did nothing to ease his pain.

He unwound the cravat from his neck and flung it aside then pounded his clenched fist on the desk. The evening had been a success—an intolerable, unbearable, blinding success.

It wasn't a horrible dream as Julian had first thought when he awakened in the leather winged-back chair in the library. The crick in his neck and the cramp in his lower back proved what was happening around him were all too real.

Lord Nathan Ellerby had entered just shortly after

Maxwell announced the visitor's punctual arrival for Lady Cassandra's afternoon drive.

The squire rose as quickly as he could manage, considering the pain running up his neck and shooting down his back.

By gad, he was tired.

Moving with some semblance of balance and grace, he made his way to the hallway just in time to see Cassandra and Ellerby leave. Maxwell opened the front door.

"And may I ask, who is to be your chaperone?" the squire called from the hallway just outside his library to the rapidly retreating forms.

"Not to worry, Squire, Romeo will be a splendid chaperone." Cassandra smiled indignantly. Romeo ran outside and jumped into the back seat of Ellerby's curricle.

Julian was not pleased with this unpleasant outcome.

"Good day to you, Maxwell." Ellerby tipped his hat in obvious good humor and ushered Cassandra out the door.

"Good day to you," the butler intoned. He stood motionless, holding the door open.

Left alone, feeling outraged, Julian stopped in the corridor and shouted, "Shut the door!"

During the remainder of the week, Julian continued to brood over Lady Cassandra's poor choice of beau. And Ellerby! He had made such a pest of himself. Calling every day. He cleverly made sure a gift of some sort preceded each of his carefully planned visits. Flowers, candies, assorted trinkets, and, just this morning, a new bonnet!

The man went so far as to bring treats for her dog!

Imagine, trying to win Cassandra's affection by offering trifles to her pet.

Surely Romeo could see through the man? But then again, Romeo was only a canine.

What bothered Julian most of all was it might just be working. Ellerby had the charm; he had wiles. What Ellerby may not have known is that Cassandra had a time limit and she would have to find someone to marry. Could Ellerby, a confirmed bachelor, come up to scratch?

This day was particularly warm, warmer than most they had experienced this summer. Lord Nathan's dark blue curricle once again waited outside Stewart Hall.

Cassie brought her parasol to fend off the strong rays of the sun. She fingered the ruffles thoughtfully, remembering Edward and the day she and Lorna had each received their gifts. It seemed so long ago . . . a lifetime ago.

"Would you mind a different route for a change?" A confident Lord Nathan had already altered the course of the curricle.

"What did you have in mind?" Cassie felt perfectly

at ease in Lord Nathan's company. He had always be-
haved as a perfect gentleman should. A change of
destination did not alarm her in the least.

"It seems frightfully warm this afternoon. I thought
we might stop for an ice." The transport passed the entrance to the park and continued down the street. "Is
that agreeable to you?" He raised an inquiring eye-
brow and waited patiently for a reaction.

Not altogether sure what "an ice" consisted of,
Cassie's response was one of indifference more than
of enthusiastic approval.

Arriving at Berkeley Square, there were obviously
others who shared the same opinion about the day's
weather.

Lord Nathan and Cassie found themselves at, liter-
ally, a standstill. Dozens upon dozens of carriages
clogged the street. Only one solitary lane was purposely left open to allow the stream of traffic to pass
through. They and all these other carriages sat parked
in the street in front of Gunther's, apparently for the
same reason.

Cassie noticed waiters darting around and about the
stationary vehicles and gasped at every near miss. The
waiters were as graceful as a dance in motion, death
defying in their precise performance. Their fleet movements and turns and their bobbing heads held the patrons who waited enthralled in a dazzling street show.

With the surrounding commotion, Cassie wasn't
aware Lord Nathan had ordered their refreshment.

Several minutes later two white current ices arrived before them, deftly delivered on a tray.

"By your expression, I take it you've never sampled these exquisite treats." Lord Nathan's statement hung in the air.

Cassie looked at the melting morsel and merely shook her head. With his spoon in hand, he asked Cassie to sample the fare with a wave.

"Delightful!" she exclaimed.

Several hours later, Lord Nathan Ellerby returned Lady Cassandra safely to Stewart Hall. He bid her a gracious good-bye and left a reference to a more than chance meeting at the Assembly Room for the following night. Maxwell stood sentry in the foyer while Lord Nathan watched Lady Cassandra ascend the staircase.

Lord Nathan took two sidesteps and leaned toward the butler. "Tell me, I don't suppose the squire is about?"

"I believe he is in the library. Do you wish me to disturb him on your behalf?"

"Exactly what I had in mind," Lord Nathan replied with a chuckle.

"If you will be so good as to remain here while I speak to the squire."

"Don't mind at all."

Maxwell inclined his head before proceeding down the hallway to inquire whether the squire was free to speak to Lord Nathan. Squire Stewart, although interested, did not seem pleased to make time for visitors. However, several minutes later, Maxwell emerged into the hallway and asked Lord Nathan to enter.

From down the hall, Miss Lorna stepped out of the small parlor and Romeo followed. The terrier made a detour and trotted down the corridor. He must have heard the pair of footsteps leading to the library. She soon followed but stopped short when she spotted Maxwell standing at the door while Lord Nathan continued into the library.

She leaned up against the wall, pulling her skirt back in an attempt to remain undetected. However, Miss Lorna's eyes lit up. A broad smile crossed her lips. She must have guessed why Lord Nathan would want to speak to her brother, as had Maxwell.

Lord Nathan was here to offer for Lady Cassandra. Miss Lorna called Romeo and ran for the stairs, no doubt to find Lady Cassandra and tell her the news. Romeo sprinted up the stairs behind the young girl, heading for his mistress' room.

"This is preposterous!" Julian bellowed. "You've only been courting Lady Cassandra for a week! How could you make such an impulsive decision?"

There wasn't much formality in Ellerby's visit. However, it did seem he wanted to proceed through the proper channels in asking permission for Cassandra's hand.

"We can't be taking our time at our age, can we, Stewart?" Ellerby strolled to the side table and perused the liquor bottles. "The young bucks will beat us out, don't you know?" He helped himself to the brandy. "Do you mind?" He didn't wait for an answer before filling a glass.

He eased into a chair and leaned back, placing his booted feet atop the desk and crossing them at the ankles. A most disgusting habit of Edward's. Julian liked it even less when Ellerby did it.

"You know, Cassandra is quite a fetching thing. Thought so the first time I laid eyes on her. I instantly regretted that she was attached to your brother." Ellerby regarded the liquid in the glass, swirling the contents. "Circumstances being what they are, I don't intend to waste any more time than need be."

Ellerby looked so sure and smug, as if he knew all the facts, which, of course, he didn't. Julian couldn't imagine Cassandra confiding in this scoundrel.

"Your brother is gone, leaving Lady Cassandra quite free, not without a hint of scandal, I might add." Ellerby punctuated his remark with a jab of his index finger. "There must have been a reason for the hasty engagement. All of which brings me here. I know exactly what I want in a wife and I am more than willing to fill Edward's shoes."

"Does Lady Cassandra fall into that category?"

"Surprisingly enough, she does. That's why I'm here to ask for her hand. Not that it's really necessary."

Julian felt his blood begin to boil. He would never allow Cassandra to marry this blackguard. Ellerby was a lying scoundrel—so arrogant and ruthless, so bloody sure of himself.

"I believe that will be enough!" the squire spat. He snatched the glass from Ellerby's hand and pushed his feet off the desk. "Get out!"

"I beg your pardon?" Ellerby protested this discourteous treatment with a tinge of surprise in his voice.

Julian became incensed. He had told himself all along he would not interfere with Lady Cassandra's choice of men. But he just could not stand by and watch—Ellerby would not have her.

"I would never consent to Lady Cassandra marrying a rogue such as you!"

"I'm no worse than your brother," he returned, leveling an equally hurtful insult.

"Get out of my house!" Julian threw the glass at the grate in anger. The glass shattered. The alcohol caused the flame to flare. "I don't want to catch you looking in Lady Cassandra's direction!"

"You sound like the jealous beau, Stewart!" Ellerby snickered and moved toward the door.

The squire roared again, "Get out!"

Chapter Ten

The squire could see Cassandra was eagerly awaiting Ellerby's arrival that next evening at the Assembly Rooms. She might find herself facing a disappointment. Julian did not expect his presence at all.

If the scoundrel had the bad judgment to attend, it would be to his advantage not to impose himself on Lady Cassandra. Julian would make certain of it.

Lord Nathan did arrive—finally. Cassie watched him enter. However, his less than warm greeting from across the room consisted of the smallest incline of his head while sporting a positively evil, distant smile.

But was that expression meant for her? Cassie wondered. She did not believe so but she had her suspicions. She turned to catch the squire's reaction. His face was unreadable, simply impenetrable.

Lord Nathan did not even show an ounce of courtesy by asking her for a dance. Cassie thought it a bit odd that he should ignore her now since he'd called nearly every day for a week. This was very strange indeed.

As it turned out, Sir Horace and Squire Stewart were the only men who asked Cassie for a dance. During the course of the evening, whenever Cassie glanced at Lord Nathan, she found him not looking in her direction but glaring at the squire.

She inclined her head toward Sir Horace when the quadrille came to an end. He escorted her off the floor and graciously thanked her for the dance.

The squire made his approach toward the couple. Sir Horace politely excused himself. Cassie felt the squire's blaring presence. His mostly hazel eyes had sharpened to a vivid green. He had tracked her every movement on the dance floor and stood watch over her.

"Did you enjoy your dance?" the squire asked.

"Very much." She stared at him with uncertainty.

"Our waltz is next," he reminded her. An uncomfortable silence hung heavy in the air. She waited for a confession from him. But she found none forthcoming.

Something had happened between the squire and Lord Nathan. The series of events this evening left her with little doubt.

When the squire caught Cassie gazing in Lord

Nathan's direction, he said, "I don't think it wise to approach Ellerby, Lady Cassandra."

"And exactly why is that, may I ask?"

"I believe the association with that fellow is at an end. You will find his interest in you has cooled."

"Has it?" she replied thoughtfully. "Will you explain why?"

"None that I care to discuss in public." A self-assured smile crossed his face.

"I suppose there is nothing to be done." Cassie gave the pretense that she had taken the squire at his word. "Would you"—she looked at him with the most sincere expression she could manage—"could you . . . if you would be so kind as to fetch me some refreshment? I find that I am ever so parched." Then she gave him a small smile.

He glanced around as if he could discover her deception. No, she was merely thirsty and she wanted to be rid of him, if only for a minute or two.

"Your servant." He acquiesced, and with a shallow bow of his head he left.

My prison guard, more like. Cassie could not imagine what had come over him or over Lord Nathan. What had happened to the men around her?

It took only a minute for the squire to return. He wasn't gone nearly as long as she would have liked. He handed her a glass of punch and, in keeping with her desperate need for liquid, she profusely thanked him.

"Cassie? Is that really you? Lady Cassandra Phillips?" The tall, dark, and handsome man called out from across the room.

She turned toward the familiar voice. "Roger Shelby!" A cheerful expression graced Cassie's face when she recognized her old friend as she passed her empty glass to the squire.

"What a most delightful surprise! Had I known of your presence, I would have dashed immediately to your side. I fear by now I must have missed my chance to stand up with you."

"Squire Stewart is promised the next dance." She threw a fleeting glance in his direction. "I'm sure he won't mind at all if you take his place." She followed the expression with a tenuous smile.

The squire nodded and bowed in resignation.

Cassandra moved to Shelby and wrapped her arm through his. Their smiles of joy made Julian all the more dismal. In her discovery of an old friend, she found a kindred heart. One that could be, he feared, more of a threat than Ellerby had been.

With his eyes glued on the retreating couple, Julian passed Cassandra's glass to Horace as he followed the couple. Unprepared to take the glass, Horace performed a minor juggling act, bouncing the fragile piece precariously from hand to hand, trying to capture the airborne culprit.

Only moments earlier, the squire had secretly

praised himself for his clever work in extinguishing Ellerby's flame. Now some *old friend* showed up, partnered Cassandra and stole his dance.

Julian lightly harrumphed. As if she would take notice of this country bumpkin.

The squire continued to watch. Cassandra's smiling eyes gazed into the simpleton's face. This . . . *Roger* may have reflected the same sentiment, although Julian would describe the expression on Cassandra's partner's face more as a dog drooling over a savory tidbit.

Julian would make certain the *friend* would not share a single minute alone with her.

That cad dare not get close enough to stroke the smooth skin of her cheek. The memory of her exquisite scent warmed him. No, Julian would not allow this stranger, no matter how familiar Cassandra made him, those exclusive liberties. The squire approached the couple.

After the dance ended, Roger silently suggested they step out on the side landing with a quick movement of his head. Cassandra smiled and nodded. She laid her hand upon Roger's arm. He placed his hand atop hers to assure safe passage off the dance floor through the French doors that led outside.

As soon as they stepped onto the terrace, Shelby half-swung Cassandra out in front of him. "How good it is to see you again!" he exclaimed.

"It has been a long time, Roger." She was glad to see a familiar, friendly face. "You must come out to Stewart Hall tomorrow to see Romeo. He's grown so."

"I don't think he could possibly stay as small as he was, considering he was the runt of the litter." Shelby laughed. "I have an appointment in the morning but I'll cancel it."

Just on the far side of the wide landing, the squire edged around the corner discreetly and remained in the shadows, eavesdropping.

Shelby drew Cassandra's hands together and planted an affectionate kiss on each.

"That will be quite enough!" Julian called out, interrupting them.

Squire Stewart stepped out into full view and shoved Roger against the balustrade, away from Cassie, and advanced toward him. Roger raised his leg, pulling his knee close to his chest, and kicked the squire across the landing, sending him to collide into one of the large potted plants that flanked the double glass doors.

The defensive maneuver compromised Roger's balance on the wide railing. He toppled over the edge, dropping onto the pathway below. Luckily, it was not far.

Cassie dashed to the balustrade and leaned over, peering down into the darkness. "Roger, dear . . . Roger, are you all right?"

"I'm fine," his weakened voice responded. "Nothing's broken as far as I can tell." But it sounded as if the wind had been knocked out of him.

Cassie spun toward the sound of the squire's approaching footfalls.

"I hope you're proud of yourself!"

"He'll soon recover, if he's any kind of a man." The squire brushed the dust from his trousers. "Now, you will come with me." He took her hand and slipped his arm around her waist, making sure she moved forward with him.

The couple stepped into the Assembly Rooms from the terrace. Their entrance drew several stares and piqued interest as they emerged from the direction where various strange sounds had originated.

With a gentle but firm guiding hand, he led Cassie through the ballroom. Their superficial smiles masked the hostility they each suppressed inside. They continued out the side doors, down the hall to a small side room. The squire closed the doors after they entered.

"How dare you drag me away!" Cassie scolded.

"I was merely providing protection. He had you quite secure in his arms. No telling what would have happened had I not intruded."

"He held my *hand*," Cassie corrected. "And how *dare* you leave him out there. He could be seriously hurt."

"He said himself that he was not injured. I'm sure some good Samaritan will hear his groans and lend

him aid." The squire cleared his throat. "I had to in-
tervene. It is not proper for you to display such inti-
macy with a stranger!"

"Roger Shelby is not a stranger."

"No matter, for propriety's sake you should not have
been alone with him," Squire Stewart's voice grew in
volume. "And you should not have invited him to
Stewart Hall without consulting me first."

Cassie moved to the liquor decanters on a credenza.
"It seems Roger and I weren't alone at all, then. You
were there the entire time—listening." She lifted the
large crystal decanter and poured the contents into a
short wide-mouthed glass.

"You do not intend to drink that, do you?" The
squire gasped, disturbed that she might imbibe.

"Certainly not. It is for you. I believe you need it
to calm you." She replaced the heavy crystal stopper.

"I don't *want* it!"

"I must insist," she said calmly. With one quick
movement of her wrist, she launched the spirit into
his face.

The squire froze. He kept his eyes closed, the
odorous liquid ran down and dripped from his face
onto his shirt, vest, and jacket then finally onto the
carpet.

"There"—she paused, reveling in the moment of
silence she'd created—"I do believe it has helped."

The drenched squire reached into his jacket and
she spotted a flash of gold from his signet ring. He

drew out a pristine white silk handkerchief and proceeded to blot the remaining moisture from his face.

Cassie's voice softened as she addressed him. "I think you need to get your priorities straight. Do you or do you not wish me to marry?"

She paused to give him a moment to think.

"Do you or do you not want me to marry? If you will not do the honor yourself, then it must be some other gentleman. It's as simple as that. I know Lord Nathan came by yesterday. I know he's already offered for me and you've said no."

She paused again, just to allow time to let her words sink into his thick skull.

"When you have regained your manners, we can discuss this further. Until that time, I suggest you enjoy your drink." She set the empty glass on the table. Turning on her heel, Cassie made a swift exit.

Julian mopped his face with his silk kerchief. As he finished, he began to think over Cassandra's words.

I did instruct her to marry. Am I standing in her way of making any match at all? And why would I do such a thing? What is it I want?

"What about me?" he murmured to himself. "Do my feelings not matter?"

Cassandra loves me. She's told me as much. Why can I not act on my feelings for her? But what were they exactly . . . he wasn't quite sure.

There was also that kiss. He could instantly conjure up and vividly recall the kiss Cassandra and he had shared.

It was the sight he saw when he closed his eyes before he fell asleep. It was the recurring dream that tortured him night after night. The memory of her warm, supple lips upon his haunted him.

Dash it all—he wanted her for himself!

He had thrown out Ellerby after his offer of marriage. Tonight he interrupted her reunion with an old acquaintance. Julian had no idea how old or how close that friendship was but he did not wish it to develop any further.

What was he doing thwarting every chance she had to marry? The truth, he discovered, was that he could not bear to see her with another. Not just Ellerby or Shelby—not any man. If he continued in this fashion, she would end up with no husband and, thus, no inheritance.

Then it dawned on him. *There was nothing wrong with his intentions.*

Julian was so caught up in his *duty* of making sure the stipulations in the earl's will were fulfilled . . . he simply did not think of the obvious solution.

With Edward's absence, it seemed the perfect solution. Their fathers wanted the families united. His marriage to her would certainly accomplish that. Although with his legal ties to the Phillips family, the union may seem odd to outsiders. What did he care?

Julian made his way down the corridor and into the

ballroom. He scanned the crowd for the violet dress Cassandra wore.

"I say, Julian, do you think it's proper to be here in your state?" Horace sniffed in the squire's direction.

Julian grabbed Horace's coat lapels. "Have you seen her, Lady Cassandra?"

"I believe I saw her leave not more than ten or fifteen minutes ago."

"Leave? Oh no!" Julian eyes shot open with panic. He needed to see her, to tell her, now.

"I thought you might be outside waiting." Horace remained calm. "Didn't think about it much really."

"She's taken my rig," the squire realized.

"By herself?" Horace chortled. "Don't be ridiculous man. She's probably caught a ride from someone else."

"No, Horace, that's not possible." The squire dragged him out of the ballroom and down the hall. "She doesn't have any friends in town."

"By the look of you I'd say she's done the impossible." Horace glanced at his friend's much altered manner.

"I need you to take me home right away!" Julian motioned for the footmen to bring their hats and coats.

"I've promised the next set to Mary Worthington," Horace balked. "I'm sure you're quite mistaken, Julian."

"We have to leave—now!"

Horace looked down at his crushed lapels. "Is all this abuse necessary?"

The squire hadn't noticed his white-knuckled fists grasping Horace's jacket. "I'm so sorry." He eased his grip and smoothed the wrinkles. "If my carriage is here, you may return to your Miss Worthington with my soundest apologies. If not, I must insist—"

"Fair enough," Horace replied.

After donning their coats, hats and gloves, the two men dashed outside.

Sure enough, the squire's carriage was missing. Once aboard Horace's chaise they started off for Stewart Hall.

Chapter Eleven

Cassie had left Squire Stewart stranded. She did not care how angry it would make him. She knew he would be resourceful enough to find a ride home. If not, the long walk would do him good.

Upon her return to Stewart Hall, she swept into her room and prepared for bed. For a few moments she kept her mind busy on her task but soon it wandered to thoughts of the squire. Confronting him tonight had not been easy. Her words had been uttered in anger, not in the loving manner that might have convinced him of her affection.

Maybe she had pushed him too far. How could she have known he would react in such an unpredictable manner? Fighting with Roger was more than she thought possible.

Poor Roger. She hoped he was not badly hurt. She had not thought to inquire about him before leaving the premises.

The squire's behavior had outraged her. Perhaps she, too, had acted rash. Dousing him with a drink was not the act of a civilized lady. If he had continued with his tirade, she didn't know to what extreme she would have retaliated.

The sound of thundering footsteps interrupted her thoughts. They grew in intensity. Seated at her dressing table, Cassie could feel the floor vibrate as someone climbed the stairs.

Lavette ran to the door and shrieked out in alarm when it flew open with such force that the handle hit the wall.

"Get out of the way." It was the unmistakable voice of Julian Stewart. "I don't care *how* she is dressed!"

"*Pardon, s'il vous plait.*" Lavette backed from the squire toward Cassie. "I must object! Zis eez no way to receive a gentleman!"

"It's quite all right. As it happens, Squire Stewart is not a gentleman," Cassie remarked, not at all surprised at his presence.

"If you please, my lady." He took a moment to draw in a breath. "I shall wait to speak to you in the library . . . at your convenience."

Julian ran down the stairs and steamed into the library. He stripped off his jacket, still reeking of spirits, and tossed it aside. It was uncomfortably warm in here. He swung open the window and tore the cravat from his neck. He unbuttoned the top buttons at the collar of his shirt and pulled away the material from his sweat-and-spirit-soaked skin, allowing the evening air to cool him.

Maxwell appeared. "Is there anything you require, sir?"

"Have tea brought in for Lady Cassandra when she arrives."

"I shall see to it at once," he said and disappeared.

Impatient for Cassandra's arrival, he could not sit and wait for her. He paced from the window to the desk and back again. He tread the well-worn path for nearly an hour and consulted his watch on an average of every three minutes.

Where the devil was she?

Cassandra stood in the doorway, a picture of calm, dressed in a simple long-sleeved blue gown with a round neckline. Her hair was bound at the neck, hung loose on her back. Short hairs formed soft curls, framing her face.

He knew better than to snap at her, demanding to know what had taken her so long. That temper of his had not done much for him this evening. He would try to restrain that beast.

"Did you wish to speak with me?" was her polite inquiry, without so much as a reference to the scene they played only an hour ago.

The squire smiled and sketched a shallow bow, bidding her welcome.

Cassandra entered the room seemingly unafraid with her hands clasped in front of her and her chin held high. A maid bustled in and left a tea tray on the table. Cassandra waited for the maid to leave before seating herself on the sofa. She remained quiet, waiting for the squire to speak.

"In all my years," he began, "I find your actions very disturbing."

"Sir, it seems that you have been out of sorts all evening." She took up her cup of tea. "Perhaps if you had some tea."

"Out of sorts? I am not out of sorts!" His hands had clenched into tight fists. "And I don't want any tea!"

"Perhaps you need a touch of sherry to calm your nerves?" She looked up at him sweetly.

A small knock sounded in the moment of silence.

Julian yelled at the door, "What is it?"

The door creaked, swinging open only a few inches. Maxwell did not enter, only leaned toward the room. "Sir? I thought perhaps there might be a problem?"

"No!" Julian had not meant to respond so abrupt. He closed his eyes and pinched the bridge of his nose. He took a breath and held it, endeavoring to gather his scattered thoughts. "Everything is fine, Maxwell, please leave us."

"Yes, sir." The butler inclined his head and retreated.

"Out of sorts," Cassandra whispered as if confirming she had been correct all along.

Perhaps she had been. "Maxwell is not used to hearing me . . . has never heard me, speak to anyone in that manner."

"You were not speaking. You were shouting, sir."

"I was not—" He broke off his sentence when he detected the volume of his voice creeping upward. Julian began again, this time with practiced calm. "I apologize for my outburst."

"Kind apology accepted." Cassandra took another sip of tea and glanced at him over the rim of the cup. Setting the cup and saucer on the mahogany table, she moved to warm herself at the fire.

"If I may be so bold, what has brought on this bout of temper?"

Julian noticed the illuminating glow from the hearth caress her face. The flickering fire sparkled in her eyes. She looked more beautiful now than ever.

He stood next to her, taking in the graceful lines of her face, the curve of her cheek, the pout of her lips. He fought the temptation to wrap his arms around her and kiss her but only for the moment.

"I must apologize for my behavior earlier this evening. I think I have finally come to terms with myself. A man of my years should know better."

"Exactly how should one of your advanced years

behave?" She stared at him with those dazzling blue eyes.

He could feel it starting. Her eyes were mesmerizing him. Just a little longer he told himself. He had to wait until the time was right.

"You know, you were quite right when you said I should know exactly what I want in life." His glance flew from her eyes to her lips and back again. "It has taken me all this time to realize exactly what I desire."

"And what is it you desire?" Her words so soft, they lingered in the air between them.

"You," he whispered. He let loose his control and gave his heart permission to act. His lips took hers. The wanting, the longing he had felt, momentarily extinguished with the touch of her lips.

Julian wrapped his arm around her, pulling her near. Cassandra's hands swept over his shirt and encircled his neck. He kissed her smooth, lightly scented cheek and trailed kisses down her neck. She sighed his name.

Cassie felt herself melting in his arms. Trapped in his embrace, she smelled a trace brandy in the air, blending with his scent. This was what she wanted, this was what she craved, this was what she had been fighting for.

"You're not pulling away." Her breathing was labored. "Do you no longer consider this wrong?"

He released her, easing back. He trapped her

hands within his. "I have tried to act indifferent as I watched you with other men. I found myself growing quite . . ."

"Jealous?" She smiled.

"I would hate to think that but I suppose you're right. It disturbed me to see your attentions being spent on other men." His hand moved to her face and he cradled her jaw. "I just never would admit to myself how much I cared for you. I've never had these kinds of feeling for anyone."

"You mean *in love*?"

"Yes." The light in his eyes glowed brighter than the fire. "Completely, madly, passionately, desperately, in love. I'm sorry it took me so long to realize. I wish to marry you, if you'll have me?"

"With all my heart." She wrapped her arms around his neck and kissed him.

"You shall be married by the end of next week." The squire delivered a tender kiss in the palm of her hand. "Just as your father wished."

A jubilant smile danced across Cassie's face. Moistness gathered in her eyes, making them sparkle even more. The tears escaped, trickling down her face.

"Why are you crying?" He frowned. "I thought this would please you?"

"They are tears of joy."

"Tears for happiness?" he mumbled and shook his head. Julian pulled her tighter to him, in a warm, comforting embrace. "I don't know if I shall ever understand women."

On a cloud of ecstasy, Cassie floated off to bed. Everything felt right, the way things were meant to be. As she donned her night rail, she realized there might be, most probably would be, some talk going around town.

She, who had been engaged to Edward, now marries his brother—the two of them living under the same roof for all these months now should rush into marriage. It didn't matter in the least. She would be spending the rest of her life with the man she loved.

Cassie sank into the soft bed and pulled the coverlet up to her smiling face. She lowered her eyelids but found the exhausting and exhilarating events of that evening did nothing to help her sleep. She lay in the dark, dreaming of what it would be like to spend a lifetime in Julian's arms and in his bed.

Julian rocked his head back and a smile of satisfaction graced the squire's lips. For the first time in his life, he was truly happy. Happy for himself, happy for Cassandra and happy for their fathers, who were not here to witness their union. From now on, life would be quite different.

A chorus of voices from out in the hallway disturbed his tranquility. Echoing though the library doors from the foyer, the mumbles became ringing cries and ecstatic shouts. Julian strode with increasing interest to the door and pulled it wide open.

"What's all this, then?"

The crowd of servants gathered in the foyer, most in their bedclothes. They parted, revealing a man.

Julian felt the blood drain from his face.

His brother Edward had returned home.

Chapter Twelve

Julian remained rooted in shock. The house servants stood around the newly returned master. Edward tried to get a word in, but couldn't manage among the enthusiastic greetings.

"Edward!" The squire's strong voice reverberated within the foyer.

It took a few minutes for the staff to calm. A path opened from Julian to his brother. Edward politely bowed at the staff, thanking them for his warm welcome. He left their protective circle and headed toward the squire.

With a smile, Edward strode past his brother and down the hallway into the library. Julian followed and closed the doors behind him.

"What the devil is going on?" the younger Stewart asked, throwing a puzzled look over his shoulder.

"You're alive," Julian whispered. He still found it hard to believe.

"Of course I am. Why shouldn't I be?" The brothers stood in silence for a few moments. "I'm afraid I still don't understand what all the to-do is about."

He lifted a decanter and poured himself a spot of brandy before dropping into a chair. Edward finished the maneuver by propping his feet on the low table in front of him.

"We all thought you were dead."

"Dead?"

"I've hired men, they're out looking for any trace of you."

"What? Don't be absurd! I haven't felt more alive in my life!" He lifted the snifter to toast his *joie de vivre* and took a generous swallow. "I don't understand. Why on earth would you think I was dead?"

"The ship you booked passage on from the continent, *King's Quest*, sank." Julian informed his obviously oblivious brother. The squire still could not believe he was here. "Why didn't you contact us? Let us know you were safe?"

"It never occurred to me. Just took a brief detour, that's all. I do it all the time. What does it matter anyway?"

"Matter?" There were times when Julian really

had difficulty understanding his brother. "There are many of us who are concerned about your welfare."

"Dead?" Edward smiled and took it all in stride. Actually, it seemed to have amused him.

Julian took on an air and announced, "With your . . . absence I had to advise Lady Cassandra to make another match and marry."

"What?" Edward dropped his feet to the floor and sprang upright in his chair.

"It is her father's wish she marry before her birthday." He clasped his hands behind his back and stepped toward Edward.

"She hasn't made a match yet has she?"

"Well, not officially." Julian expected their recent plans were now at an end.

"The reason I postponed my departure home was to take a side trip to purchase an engagement present for her." Edward reached into his inside coat pocket and produced a dark green velvet box. Pulling open the lid he unveiled an emerald ring. "Do you think she'll like it?"

The squire gasped at the gaudy gem. "Don't you think it's a trifle . . . imposing?"

"Lady Cassandra deserves the best." Edward closed the velvet box and placed it in the safety of his coat pocket, next to his heart.

"That, my brother, is one subject we can both agree on."

*   *   *

Cassie awoke to a glorious morning. The streaming rays of the sun bathed her room with natural light. She stretched her arms overhead, allowed them to drop back on the feather pillows and gave a satisfying yawn.

Was last night really as wonderful as she remembered or was it all a dream? As she recalled, she and Julian had finally admitted they loved one another. Today, they would begin to plan their future.

This was more than she could ever imagine. Her life was perfect. Cassie had never, ever felt happier than at this very moment.

"*Bonjour*, my lady!" Adorned with a cheerful smile, Lavette entered the bedchamber with a tea tray. She brought her mistress a cup of chocolate.

"It is a lovely morning, Lavette." For once Cassie found herself in full agreement with her maid.

"The news, she eez wonderful, *n'est-ce pas*?"

Cassie began to come out of her enchanted daydream. "News? What news?" Surely no one yet knew about her and Julian.

However, she wasn't entirely sure that the squire would wait to make any declaration of that kind. He had been known to be rather hasty when it came to making wedding announcements.

Cassie pulled back the covers and swung her legs over the edge of the bed. Stepping into her satin slippers, she took the morning chocolate from Lavette.

"The entire house—*she* has been speaking of nothing else! *C'est* miracle!"

Cassie sipped from the cup. Her marrying Julian was wonderful—a dream come true—but a miracle? "What are you talking about?"

"You shall never have to put up with *de comportement de cet homme detestable!*" Lavette referred to the squire's reprehensible behavior of last night, barging into her ladyship's boudoir. *"Monsieur Edward est de retour!"*

The cup handle slipped from Cassie's fingertips. It crashed onto the saucer, knocking it from her hand, and landed on the hardwood floor.

"Mon Dieu!" Lavette raced to retrieve the porcelain shards scattered around Cassie's feet.

"What's that you say?" A blank look replaced the joyful expression that had once graced Cassie's face. Her French wasn't what it should be and she thought, hoped actually, that she had misinterpreted her maid's answer.

"Monsieur Edward, he eez alive! He has come home!" She knelt and carefully placed the porcelain pieces in a cloth napkin. "He returned late last night after you had gone to bed. Did you not know?"

Cassie felt her heart sink into a deep, dark dreadful place. *Could it really be true?*

"Lavette, I need to dress at once!"

"You wish to look *tres belle, n'est-ce pas?*" Lavette smiled.

"It doesn't matter . . . quickly!" She dashed to her dressing table to start her hasty toilette.

Lavette made a final wipe of the floor, moved to the closets in the next room and rummaged through the day dresses to find her favorite.

"Which will we choose?" Lavette lightly fingered each dress as she contemplated the choice.

"Plus vite, Lavette!"

Lavette brought in a cerulean morning dress. She took a brush and began to style Cassie's hair. "I think we should pull eet up, just zo?" Lavette gazed at her mistress' reflection in the large mirror and cocked her head to one side, pondering the overall effect.

"Never mind! Just bind it!" Cassie gathered her hair at the base of her neck. Lavette tied the mass with a matching light blue ribbon.

"I, too, would be anxious to see Monsieur Edward! I shall keep you no longer!"

Placing one brave foot ahead of another, Cassie neared the stairs, composing herself for whatever the truth was and whatever consequence it would have on her future. She descended with poise.

Continuing down the hallway, she stopped when she saw Lorna collapse in the doorway of the library. Edward Stewart moved at an alarming rate, gathered his sister in his arms and carried her delicate body into the room.

Cassie found herself at the doorway, staring intensely at the apparition before her. It was the only explanation—he must have been a ghost.

Edward could not have returned from the dead, but there he stood—flesh and blood at his sister's side.

"Here, use this." A familiar signet ring-adorned hand intruded into the picture, handing Edward a vinaigrette. Cassie's gaze followed the hand to Julian's face.

The squire's gaze met hers. It was not the look of joy it had been last night.

Lorna stirred; she moaned softly. Her eyes opened, stared at Edward.

"It is you! I thought I was going mad!" Lorna sat up and wrapped her arms around her brother's neck, welcoming him with an enormous hug. "Cassie! Look! Edward has returned. He's alive—just as Julian said!"

Edward freed himself from his sister's affectionate embrace and stood, facing Cassie. "I do beg your pardon." He rushed to her side. "I did not mean to . . . I had not realized that my return would cause such a stir."

Edward took both of Cassie's hands and planted a kiss on each. Then drawing her near, he repeated the performance on each of her pale cheeks.

"I never intended to cause distress to anyone with my small delay home. Most of all you, my dear."

Cassie thought she should say something. As his betrothed, she should have been overjoyed by his homecoming. At least relieved that he was still alive.

But Cassie felt numb.

"It's a miracle," she managed. "I can hardly believe you're really here."

"Yes, more anxious than ever to marry you," Edward assured her.

Cassie's breath stopped in her throat. However she did manage a smile. "You must excuse me. This entire episode has taken its toll on me." It was true, her stomach began to feel upset.

"My apology, how insensitive I've been. Please, sit down." He walked her to the sofa, setting her next to Lorna who by now had quite recovered. "Let me send for breakfast."

"No, thank you, I'm not hungry," Cassie replied.

"Just tea, then?" Edward nodded to Maxwell, who stood silently in the doorway. The butler retreated and saw to the request.

Mrs. Upton proved more delicate than her sturdy appearance suggested and fainted dead away when she set eyes upon the younger Stewart brother. It took both Edward and the squire to drag her to the sofa and prevent her from foundering to the floor.

A moment later, Maxwell entered with a tea tray for the ladies.

"I hope it's strong," commented Mrs. Upton, recovered from her spell. She still couldn't tear her eyes off Edward.

"You told me he was alive, Julian! You promised you'd find him and here he is!" Lorna giggled. Nothing could have made her happier than her brother's unexpected presence.

Maxwell once again stood at the doorway. "Lord Ansley has arrived, sir."

Julian launched out of his chair. "Tell him I shall be with him momentarily." He nodded to the family and, most noticeably, did not glance at Cassie. "If you will please excuse me."

Anxious to remove himself from this uncomfortable situation, Julian had avoided meeting Cassandra's eyes for fear everyone would read the regret and longing he felt for her.

He glanced over his shoulder and could see that she followed him to the doorway. Her gaze met his. In that one moment, they concurred that their future together was over. The squire hurried behind Maxwell out of the front door.

Cassie felt Edward come up behind her. He cupped her elbow and edged her out into the hallway.

"Cass, I haven't told you just how much I've missed you." He leaned toward her for a kiss and with a sharp turn of her head, Cassie displaced Edward's wanton lips to her cheek.

She sighed at the near miss.

However, Edward did not take the evasion as a simple defeat. He applied a second sweet, soft kiss on the side of her neck. "I don't find the darkened corridors conducive to expressing my affection. Would you mind slipping into the side parlor with me?"

He took her by the hand. Quietly they moved down the hallway. Romeo trotted behind them. With the tip of his boot, Edward blocked Romeo's entrance. "That will assure me some privacy." He pulled the parlor door closed, preventing the terrier from joining them.

Edward sat on the sofa, pulling Cassie next to him.

"I missed you so very much. There wasn't a day that went by that I did not think of you. I cannot tell you how much it pained me to extend my absence, but the side trip I took was for your benefit."

He pulled out a small package, wrapped with gold paper and red ribbon.

"This is very special." He smiled and she could feel that he was eager for her to open her gift.

Cassie tried to muster some excitement and managed a smile. She removed the ribbon and opened the package—a container of perfume.

"Not just any scent. It is made from jasmine flowers from the East. I reserve this brand only for my wife." He chose his words with great effort. "I wish you to wear this on our wedding day. Here, allow me." Edward pulled the stopper and touched the end to the inside of her wrist. He inhaled the blend of perfume on her skin and closed his eyes, savoring the fragrance. "Lovely."

She saw the ardor in his eyes, felt the eagerness in his touch. He meant this—all of this. His sincerity, his affection, it was all real.

Not only would he marry her, he wanted to marry her. And her thoughts and feelings for him could have never been more removed.

Edward pulled out a small dark green velvet box. He rolled it around in the palm of his hand, fingering the soft fabric as he spoke. "I found this for you. A jewel for my jewel." He opened the box and Cassie stared at the opulent green gem. "It's the only one I felt was worthy of adorning your lovely finger." He removed it from its pillow and slipped it onto the third finger of her left hand.

Cassie began to cry. Changing her mind, turning him away was not possible. It was her duty to marry him.

"Do not fret. I completely understand." Edward pulled Cassie against his shoulder and stroked her back to calm her. "They are tears of joy!"

The tears slipping down Cassie's cheeks were far from joyful.

Cassie finished crying in her room. She was not aware of how much time had passed before she heard a knock on the door. An hour? Several?

The door opened slightly when she did not respond. "I'm sorry to disturb you, your ladyship," the butler said.

"Yes, Maxwell?"

"A visitor has just arrived and is waiting in the front parlor." Maxwell entered and offered her the guest's calling card.

"Roger!" She had forgotten all about her old friend and leaped to her feet. Before leaving the room, she stepped in front of the mirror for a quick check. Cassie tried to wipe the traces of tears away and pinched her cheeks for color. She knew Roger would not be fooled, but it was all she could do on such short notice.

Cassie strode into the front parlor, creating the best appearance of gaiety she could manage. Roger graciously bowed and extended a greeting that she returned.

Lorna and Romeo met them just behind the house.

"You were quite right. I believe Romeo has grown," Roger said in fun. "He's at least twice the size he was as a pup."

Cassie threw an icy glare his way. He always had something pointed to say about her pet. When she chose Romeo out of the litter, Roger had urged her to pick a stouter, more substantial animal that might amount to more than a walking slipper.

"Did you know Romeo when he was a puppy?" Lorna asked.

"Mr. Shelby bred him," Cassie explained. "He is trying to create a new breed of dog."

"I'd like to take the larger hunters and refine them into a smaller, more domesticated pet." He turned to Cassie and continued to riddle her. "But don't think I would ever try to recreate a 'Romeo.'" The terrier bounded around the visitor. Roger lifted the dog and scratched him.

Cassie could tell by Lorna's expression she took offense to this man poking fun at such a small defenseless animal.

"Romeo is simply the smartest, most splendid animal I know!" Lorna stomped her foot in outrage. "You'd do all of England a true service if there could be more like him."

Roger smiled and seemed quite delighted. "And from whom am I receiving this blistering set-down?"

"Miss Lorna Stewart, may I present Mr. Roger Shelby." Cassie nodded in Roger's direction. "Mr. Shelby, may I present Miss Lorna Stewart."

"It appears that you may not be happy to make my acquaintance but I am delighted to make yours." Roger sketched a bow. "Well, Miss Lorna I hate to admit it in Lady Cassandra's presence, but Romeo has the exact traits that I wish to propagate," he whispered for all to hear.

Lorna perked up in excitement. "Do you mean to tell me he's the first of his breed?"

"Well, nearly. I wouldn't go so far as to say there is a breed."

"Oh, that's so exciting. What are you calling them?"

"For the time being I just refer to them as York-shire Terriers."

"Oh, that is clever, Roger," Cassie said dryly. "A man from Yorkshire who breeds a new type of terrier calls the breed *Yorkshire* Terrier. Very clever."

"What can I say?" He gave a small shrug and bent, allowing Romeo to jump to the floor. The terrier dashed to the door and back toward the garden again, looking expectantly for his mistress and the visitor to follow.

"Romeo wants to go for a run," Cassie announced. "Shall we move to the rear gardens?"

"I'm afraid I cannot join you," Lorna said, briefly saddened. Then her tone lightened. "Thomas Went-worth will be arriving shortly. We're going for a drive this afternoon and we're expected to meet with Belinda and Jeffrey. I must start my toilette. A pleasure to make your acquaintance, Mr. Shelby." With that she left.

Romeo led Cassie and Roger away from the back of the house. Once they moved past the fountain, the canine dashed headlong for the back lawn.

Roger waited until they were a respectable distance from the house so they could not be overheard. "Now, would you mind telling me what is wrong? You look positively dreadful."

Knowing Roger could see her misery through her

happy facade reduced Cassie to tears. As they continued to walk, Roger placed his arm around her shoulders for comfort.

"Dear Roger, if you only knew." She pulled out her handkerchief and sobbed.

"I'm listening. Do start from the beginning and tell me everything."

Cassie began the tale with her engagement to Edward. Then how the difficulties she had to endure with Julian Stewart had unexpectedly blossomed into love after Edward's presumed death. Last night, she and Julian had decided to marry.

Last night, she had retired knowing her happiest days were those to come. When she woke, her dreams with Julian had vanished with Edward's unexpected return.

They had settled on a bench shaded by a rose-covered arbor. Roger held Cassie's hand in his.

"You are in love with the squire, aren't you?"

Cassie nodded while crying into her handkerchief. She blotted her eyes and sniffed in preparation to speak. "I must marry Edward. If I don't, I lose everything. Papa saw to that."

"Then your cousin Robert would inherit Hedgeway Park, wouldn't he? He already has your father's title and all of its holdings. I can't imagine why your father would do that to you."

"It was his dearest wish that our families be connected," she stated firmly. "Only he isn't here to see how unhappy I am. I'm sure he would understand if he were still alive."

"What are you going to do?"

Cassie blinked up at him. "I will marry Edward." This started a second flood of tears. "I'm sorry to be such a watering pot, Roger."

He pulled Cassie toward him and wrapped his arms around her. "I'm sorry to hear of your misfortune, my darling." In the motion of a mother comforting a child, he rocked her from side to side. "You know I would do anything to help." He held her away from him. "Shall I whisk you away from here and save you by marrying you myself? You know I would do that."

"That's awfully kind of you. If I married you, I would sit in Shelby Manor and every day look across the south field and see my beloved Hedgeway Park. It would be a constant reminder that I've lost my family estate along with everything else." She dabbed at her eyes and mustered some composure. "Edward is not a horrible person, you understand. He is all that is kind and very amiable." She looked hopefully into Roger's eyes. "He says we can move there after we're married. So you see, things won't be all that bad."

"I shall stay in London as long as you need me. I can come see you every day."

"No. My life's path has already been decided for me. There is no use ruining your life as well." Cassie gave a final sigh. "I should be back at home before the end of the year. I will see you at Christmas perhaps."

"Are you sure?"

"I promise. I will be fine."

After Roger's departure, Cassie retreated to her room. There, in solitude, she tarried for the remainder of the day. She refused her meals and saw no one. In her saddened state she fell asleep.

Cassie dreamt of Julian, of him holding her close, of his kisses. She could feel the cool caress of the night air on her back. She felt his hot breath moving down the side of her neck.

Cassie drew back from him with a gasp. She turned to warn her love with a single look. Instead of gazing into Julian's eyes, she found herself staring with shock at the green eyes of Edward, who now held her tight.

Covered in perspiration, Cassie jolted awake, breathing heavily from the dream and its frightening conclusion.

The afternoon was nearly at an end by the time Edward headed toward the library with a large leather pouch in hand. Walking into the room, he unfastened the protective flap and reached into it, drawing out a bundle of folded paper.

"These are the purchase agreements." Edward unfolded the thick packet of paper. "I must say we did quite well. Hefty profits." He glanced at the figures before he tossed the papers onto the unoccupied desk.

A strange silence filled the air. Edward turned to-ward the hearth. The back of his brother's favorite chair faced him.

"Julian? Julian, are you quite all right?" Edward peered around the winged-back chair.

Edward's eyes widened and he gasped at the sight of his sibling. There he saw the ever immaculate Julian Stewart sprawled in the seat. His thick, wavy hair was disheveled. One leg draped over the arm of the chair. The neck of his shirt gaped open, his shirt-tails were pulled out of his pants and wadded up in a bunch.

Julian's glazed eyes stared into the dancing flames of the hearth. The ever changing scenery of the log provided more than enough entertainment in his present condition.

"Julian? Julian?" Still Edward did not get an answer.

The squire's head snapped up from his chest. "What?"

"Are you ill?"

"Ill? No, not really. Just burning the midnight oil," he said toward the fire.

"But it's two in the afternoon."

"Two you say? And afternoon already?" The squire blinked as if waking from sleep.

"Julian, are you quite sure you're not unwell?" Ed-ward regarded his brother with a tilt of his head.

"Nonsense!" Julian straightened as best he could

in the chair, allowing his suspended leg to drop to the floor. "I am quite well, thank you. Just working a bit later than usual. Someone's got to keep an eye over the family business. Someone's got to be responsible." Moving to the side table, he rummaged through his desk drawers.

"You are behaving most peculiar." Edward remarked and continued to stare. "What has happened?"

"What's happened, you ask?" Julian straightened and faced his brother. "What's happened? Why, you've returned home safe and sound." He gestured with his arms open wide and a smile to match. "All is right in the world!" With that dramatic display at an end, he frowned, turned back to the desk and continued his search in the adjacent cabinet.

"All right, I just came to deliver these documents and tell you of the surprise I've arranged for Cass."

"Good gad, Edward! How could you possibly surprise her any more than you have?"

"I've found a new mount I think she'll fancy. Going to fetch the mare myself. Julian, you will be all right, won't you? You do plan on getting some sleep?"

"Sleep? Don't be absurd. Of course I'll get some sleep. Later, later." Julian heard the words coming out of his mouth. They slurred, sounding as if he'd been drinking. "I just have some work to finish up."

Sleep? He did not want to sleep. Closing his eyes, he saw her. Cassandra. If he dared to fall asleep he'd no doubt dream of her.

"What *are* you searching for?" Edward might have been concerned for his brother but it was difficult for Julian to tell.

The squire straightened and blinked. He could not remember. He strode back to the hearth and dropped back into his comfortable chair.

"Julian, really . . ." Edward sounded seriously fretful at his brother's bizarre state.

"Leave me alone!" Julian shouted. "You've got everything now. Don't bother yourself with my doleful welfare." The squire's sedate gaze returned to the grate and settled on the scenery of flickering flames.

Chapter Thirteen

It was very early the next morning when Maxwell presented Edward with a letter. The trace floral scent wafted to his discriminating nose. A missive from the fair Victoria Perkins, if the butler was correct.

Edward broke the seal and read the contents. The message sent a smile across his lips. "Maxwell, have my horse brought 'round. I've got to dash into town." He slapped his hand with the letter, sending waves of the lavender scent through the air.

Maxwell acknowledged with a respectful nod and, without a word, saw to the request.

"But a bit of sustenance before I leave." Edward headed to the breakfast room. After visiting the sideboard no less than three times, the young master was ready to depart. He left the house without a word as to where, or how long, he would be gone.

Maxwell noted that the squire, who had spent a second night in the library hard at work, occupied the sofa this morning. One arm dangled onto the floor while the other lay draped across his chest. One of his legs hung over the back, the other fell over the arm of the divan. As of yet, he had not seen the morning rays of the sun.

And Lady Cassandra had not come out from her room. Nor had Maxwell expected that she would without sufficient motivation.

There was a strong knock on the front door. Opening the door, a young and noticeably nervous Jeffrey Rutherford stood torturing the brim of his stylish hat.

"I've come to call on Miss Stewart," he announced in a soft and timid voice.

Maxwell stepped back, pulling the door wider to allow the young man to enter. Mr. Rutherford's nervous eyes came to rest on the silent butler, who held out the salver for his pending action.

The young man fumbled around his coat pockets, looking for his card. He placed one on the tray and smiled with confidence.

"Would you care to wait in the front parlor, sir?"

"Why, yes of course."

Maxwell led Mr. Rutherford in the direction of the yellow front parlor where he sat on the sofa and proceeded to study the room's decor. Maxwell departed to deliver the calling card.

Mrs. Upton answered the light rap at Lorna's door. Miss Lorna sat at her dressing table checking each curl and making sure her flawless face was no less than perfect.

"There is a young man belowstairs for you, miss." Maxwell's words were evenly modulated, his tone unpretentious.

"Oh! That's Jeffrey!" Lorna stood in excitement and raced for the card.

"I've put him in the front parlor." Maxwell's statuesque posture never wavered while he delivered his message.

With a dreamy smile, she read the name engraved on the card. "The Honorable Jeffrey Rutherford."

Lorna gently placed the card next to her hair brush and headed for her bonnet which was held by Mrs. Upton.

"Now, now . . ." The governess pulled the hat out of reach. "You mustn't appear too anxious. And you should make him wait. Just a bit."

"Pish-tosh! Jeffrey said he would call at three and it's just that now," she snapped, behaving quite missish. "I'll not have him think I'm a spoiled brat!" She snatched the bonnet out of Mrs. Upton's hands. With a lift of her pert nose, she turned for the door. "Do you intend to come or shall I go alone?"

"Not as long as there's a King of England!" the governess bristled, and promptly followed. "I would never hear the end of it if the squire found out you were unchaparoned," she harangued, following her charge down the corridor.

Mrs. Upton followed Miss Lorna to the parlor. Soon the sound of clicking nails on the floor announced Romeo's arrival.

"You would make a splendid chaperone, wouldn't you, Romeo?" she quipped as though Mrs. Upton were not present.

"Not likely," the governess grumbled, but not so quiet that Lorna could not hear.

Mr. Rutherford noticed Miss Lorna and Romeo appear simultaneously in the doorway of the parlor. He stood and made an extravagant, sweeping bow.

"Miss Stewart." A nervous smile danced on his face but his devotion was genuine.

"Shall we be off?" Miss Lorna donned her bonnet.

"At this very moment?" Mrs. Upton balked at the abruptness of her charge.

"If we wish to appear in the park during the fashionable hour we must leave at once," Miss Lorna announced.

Mrs. Upton rolled her eyes toward the heavens.

"We shan't be late!" Mr. Rutherford promised, eager to please the young miss.

"No need to hurry, there is ample time." Mrs. Upton waved her hand to slow him but he gestured for Miss Lorna to lead the way.

"Do you mind terribly if Romeo comes along with

us?" Miss Lorna's sweet voice lilted with a magical quality.

"Romeo?" he repeated uncertainly. The terrier circled, balanced on his hind legs and barked twice. Realizing Romeo was the dog, young Jeffrey leaned down and patted the top of his furry head. "He's a fine fellow, isn't he? All right, come along then."

Romeo dashed ahead of Miss Lorna and leaped into the waiting carriage. Mrs. Upton shared the back seat with Romeo while Miss Lorna sat next to her gentleman in the front. Mr. Rutherford took the ribbons and asked the two bays to move off toward their destination. Without a doubt it was to be Hyde Park.

Maxwell pushed the massive front door shut and stood contemplating for a moment. With Mr. Edward absent, Miss Lorna, Mrs. Upton and Romeo all gone, an idea inspired the butler.

"My deepest apology, squire," Maxwell spoke in his most dismal tone. "It seems there has been serious damage in the east wing. I cannot say whether it will be habitable in time for the upcoming wedding."

The wedding. Julian could not stand to hear one more word about *the wedding.* "Surely Maxwell, you can handle the details of the repair?" He really did not want to be bothered.

Maxwell stood rooted. "I'm afraid, this matter will require your personal attention."

Julian raked his hands through his tousled hair. "This is not like you at all, Maxwell. You usually have matters well in hand." He set his quill aside and rose to leave.

"I am sorry to disappoint you, sir. I will endeavor to make certain I am more diligent in applying myself in the future."

With candelabrum in hand, Maxwell led the way through the musty east wing. The squire knew he could hardly be trusted in his condition to carry the lit candles. One false move and the house could easily catch fire.

Julian managed the stairs well enough and grumbled at the inconvenience of this journey the entire way through the long forgotten corridors of the stately manor. He lagged behind the butler, dragging his feet along the worn carpet. A cloud of dust billowed up, leaving a wake.

The squire followed Maxwell through room after room, losing count after the first six. Julian nearly collided with him when Maxwell stopped and abruptly stepped aside.

Ahead, a single taper burned bright. In a small darkened sitting room, which at one time was grand and was now run down, stood Cassie.

The gentle illumination from the candle caressed her face. She pulled her shawl tight around her and stared at him, unblinking.

"Cassie . . ." he whispered. Julian stepped forward and reached out to her, then hesitated. "What . . . how do you come to be here?"

"Maxwell told me Romeo had wandered in this direction. I came to look for him."

It occurred to Julian that the butler who, it seemed, had orchestrated this clandestine meeting was now nowhere to be seen. He and Cassie were quite alone.

The squire chuckled. "Maxwell, dear Maxwell." He shook his head and grinned. It had been the first that had crossed his face in days.

The dark circles under Cassie's eyes told him she was not dealing with Edward's return any better than he. Julian wanted to comfort her but didn't know what to say. He wanted to touch her but was afraid she was another dream and would vanish. He wanted to hold her but knew if he did he would never let her go.

"I'm afraid I don't understand." She looked bewildered, confused.

"He's doing what he's always done—looking after me." Julian took Cassie's candlestick and set it on a small covered table off to one side.

"Are you saying Maxwell planned this?"

"He knows how miserable I've been these past few days. I have been. Very miserable." He finally admitted it not only to himself but to the woman he loved.

The longing to touch her reminded him he was

still, painfully, alive. Julian could not help himself. "I am sorry." He stepped near and cupped her face with his palm.

She leaned into his hand sending a stream of warm tears to run onto his palm. He felt her tremble beneath his touch. His fingers ran down the length of her arm, encompassing her clenched fist, quieting her shaking hand.

His thumb brushed her soft lower lip. He traced the gentle curves of her mouth. A mouth with lips he knew well. Julian swallowed hard.

"Please . . . don't . . ." She tried to resist.

Although it felt right, there would be no inappropriate actions, no crossing the lines of decorum. He told himself he would act properly.

Julian leaned forward.

Cassie closed her eyes. She parted her lips with anticipation. She waited for the warmth of his lips to comfort her. The kiss she longed for never came.

He rested his forehead on hers and ran his cheek along hers. Cassie felt the whiskers on his face scratch her. It must have been days since he'd shaved. His arms held her close in a warm, comforting embrace. She laid her head on his chest and listened to the sound of his heart.

Cassie felt him raise her hand and watched him gaze upon the obtrusive ring adorning her left hand.

"I see you're wearing his *gift*."

"It's a bit much but he meant well." The large gem

glittered with ease in the dim candlelight. Tears filled her eyes again. "Whatever are we to do?"

"There is nothing we *can* do," Julian admitted. "You must marry Edward. We both know that." He drew back and placed a gentle kiss on her forehead. "I want you to know how very much I love you." He gazed into her moist eyes. "I shall *always* love you."

"Even after I'm married to your brother?"

"I'm afraid so," he whispered. "For the honor of our families, it is our duty."

"I suppose you're right." Squeezing her eyes closed, a new flood of tears streamed down her face. Julian brushed the moisture away with the tips of his fingers.

"We must be brave. For your sake, for mine, and for Edward's."

A discreet cough came from the corner of the room. "I hate to disturb you, sir." Maxwell stood in the doorway, appearing out of nowhere. "I came to inform you that your brother has returned."

"He's back?" Cassie panicked at the slightest chance of Edward catching her alone with his brother. "I must go at once." She tore herself away from the man she loved, swept up her taper, and pushed past the butler, fleeing the room.

Silence took her place. Julian wasn't sure what he should do next.

"Your brother is currently occupied at the stables and wished to see you when he is finished. I've explained to him you were inspecting the east wing."

"I'll be right down. Maxwell?" Julian called before the butler could leave.

"Sir?"

"Thank you." But the two small words did not convey anywhere near the gratitude he felt.

"I'm sure I don't know what for," was the humble servant's reply.

"Now, keep your eyes closed. No peeking." Edward walked backwards, leading Cassie with both hands, making sure she didn't lift an eyelid and ruin his surprise.

Cassie could feel the outdoor breeze against her face. The gravel crunched under her feet as she moved forward. The smell of horses filled the air.

"All right. We're going to stop here." Edward stopped and walked behind her. "Let me take your hands and put them"—he took Cassie by her wrists—"here."

Cassie's palms rested against something smooth, soft, and warm. Under her fingers, she felt a finely groomed fur coat. At the exquisite feeling, she gasped and opened her eyes.

A beautiful bay stood before her. The mare's soft nose quivered as she nickered a welcome. A delicately arched neck displayed a healthy bushy black mane. She had large, expressive brown eyes that were said to mirror a horse's intelligence.

"She's yours," Edward said. "I hope we'll have many morning rides ahead of us."

Gently sloped shoulders, strong legs and a well-muscled body showed that the overall physical tone of the mare was excellent. Most important, her disposition was sweet. The mare stood quiet all during the inspection.

"She's lovely," Cassie said. A smile tugged at her lips. How could she not be favorably impressed? Edward never ceased to amaze her with his thoughtfulness. Unfortunately his generosity could not buy her heart. "Thank you."

"A lovely horse for a lovely lady," Edward eyed his conquest—Cassie. "Are you ready to give her a try? You're not dressed for it but we can take her for a short outing, just around the yard."

The mare was saddled at once. Cassie stepped up onto the mounting block and climbed into the saddle.

Placing the toe of his boot in the iron, Edward swung onto his horse. He led the way from the stables and down the road.

"You're looking quite pale, my dear," Edward said, riding alongside. "It's just as well you've a new mount. You should try to get out into the sun more."

Cassie forced a smile and agreed. Her morning rides with Julian had come to an abrupt end. She wasn't good company, not for anyone. Cassie had kept to herself since Edward's reappearance, becoming a recluse in her room.

"She has a nice trot. I won't have to work at sitting her," Cassie remarked as they changed gaits. "What's her name?"

"What would you like to call her?"

"What about Lady?"

Attentive and charming as ever, Edward had lavished compliments and gifts upon her since his return. It appeared that his feelings during his long absence had not changed one iota. While Cassie's most certainly had.

"I nearly forgot, *that* came for you a while back." Julian ran the sweet-scented envelope under his nose then dropped it on the table where Edward sat. "I suppose it's from one of your many admirers. You'd better take care of it. See that you end it right away."

"I see you've managed to get a few hours sleep. Your mood's much improved." Edward didn't bother to partake in the delicate fragrance and broke the seal. He nearly sprayed coffee across the table in response.

"What is it?" the squire asked, concerned.

"Nothing really." Edward blotted the beads of sweat that appeared on his upper lip with his napkin. "Well, I'm surprised that you're right, that's all. It's from an amour—an ex-amour. I guess Cass has taught you a thing or two about women during my absence."

Indeed, she had. Cassandra had done far more than that.

"I've got to handle this straight away and set this young lady to right." Edward waved the missive and headed toward the door. "No use dangling after me. I'm happily taken."

Chapter Fourteen

Cassie's tear-streaked face stood testament to the long hours she wept. It was time to get on with her life. Forget the unhappiness, forget the pain, forget the squire. Tonight Edward's aunt Lady Cowper had planned a party in honor of his return.

There would be no begging off. Cassie had to attend. She would have to face Edward and all the guests with a smile. She would have to face Julian and what?

She needed to control herself. Cassie wanted to portray the happiness she knew Edward felt. He deserved that much. She wasn't sure how, but she was determined to match his exuberance.

Lavette helped Cassie dress in an emerald-green taffeta gown. As the maid arranged her hair, Cassie regarded her pale reflection in the glass. Edward had been right, she had lost all her natural coloring. She was as pale as the simple string of pearls she wore. She dipped into the rouge pot and applied the smallest amount to her cheeks and a bit of paint to her lips, simulating their natural shade.

That evening, Cassie and Edward drove to the Cowper residence alone. She was eternally grateful that Julian had chosen to drive separately. She wasn't sure she could spend time with him in the close proximity of a coach—even if Edward was present. She told herself this was the first perfect evening of her perfect future.

When Cassie arrived, she did not search the premises for the squire. She would concentrate on Edward which meant keeping company with Edward, dancing with Edward, and laughing with Edward.

However, she felt the squire's presence the moment he arrived. He stood at the entrance to the glittering, grand ballroom and she could not help herself from looking up at him.

Julian never looked more striking. The dark blue cutaway stretched over his broad shoulders and his tan pantaloons accentuated his long legs. This must be the latest manifestation of his current valet, Postlewait.

Julian's smile gave Cassie reason to smile. She glanced about, wondering if anyone had observed her reaction.

No, no one seemed to notice.

Edward placed Cassie's hand in the crook of his arm and led her to the other side of the room. Passing through the guests, felicitations surged from well-wishers for their upcoming nuptials.

Edward and Cassie met Julian and Lorna at the bottom of the grand staircase.

"Dear sister, you resemble a goddess," Edward crooned. "Comparable only to my lovely bride."

Lorna blushed.

"I hear the waltz beginning and I believe we are long overdue for our dance." Edward extended his arm to his sister. "If you will excuse me, my dear." He gave Cassie a regal nod before heading for the dance floor.

Throughout the evening, Cassie alternately kept company with Edward and the squire. She had a better time than she ever thought possible.

Removing to the terrace, Cassie stood alone. If Julian could maintain an impenetrable exterior, so could she. Their love seemed as if it were a dream. Their kiss as if it had happened ages ago.

This was a new life, her life with Edward.

"Am I disturbing you?"

Cassie peered over her shoulder. There stood Julian. The moonlight cast a shadow across his face, sculpting his prominent nose and classic, handsome profile.

"Not at all."

He stepped into the cool night air. "You see, we can do it," the squire encouraged. "We can still be friends."

"Yes." She smiled. "I suppose we can contrive." And at that moment perhaps they both believed it.

He knew that being alone with her may not have been wise. But he was quick to extinguish the warning.

He *wanted* to be alone with her and he would have accepted any excuse he might possibly grasp. He wanted only to share her company.

"The evening has gone well, don't you think?" He gave himself permission to gaze at her. Any man would have taken the same opportunity.

He wanted only to look upon her.

The golden curls atop her head, soft and shimmering, the halo of an angel. For truly, in his eyes, she was an angel.

"I thought so." She met his appreciative stare.

Julian hadn't steeled himself for that. Not her catching him at a vulnerable moment of admiration. Now he had to face her and those eyes. Again, those eyes.

The guests and the music from the ballroom had disappeared. All he knew was the two of them, here, together in the night's air.

The counterfeit, warm smile faded from his face, his breathing deepened. Julian gazed into her alarmed eyes. He knew she could feel what was happening between them. He could no longer hold his ground and began to near.

"I'm afraid I can't help myself any longer," he whispered. Julian swept Cassie into his arms and brushed his lips against hers.

He wanted only one kiss.

"We cannot," she whispered but her tone held regret and longing. "Please—"

Was that a summons for him to continue or a plea for him to cease action?

"We mustn't . . . If someone should see us . . . You must stop . . ." She glanced into the ballroom, afraid that someone had seen them.

He stepped back, placing a considerable bit of distance between them. A wayward breeze between them cooled his ardor.

"I beg your pardon. I am very sorry, I—"

"There is no excuse. We cannot . . . there would be a scandal if we were found!"

He took another step back. Clearly he could not be trusted in her proximity. He couldn't even trust himself.

"You must promise me," she implored him. "We deny our feelings because it is what we must do, do we not?"

"It is our duty to continue."

"But we must be successful. You must help me." Tears filled her eyes, making them glisten in the moonlight. "You know that I never wished to marry Edward. I believe I made that clear the day I arrived at Stewart Hall."

·

Julian almost smiled as he remembered her slapping him. He never imagined they'd end up in a situation such as this.

"Even though marriage to Edward is not what I desire"—she paused and Julian felt his heart break as he stood before her—"I am willing do so."

It would be more difficult for him than for her. She would have Edward to love her. After the wedding they would move to her beloved Hedgeway Park.

In a year's time the squire was certain that Lorna would marry. Which left Julian alone, trapped in the mausoleum of Stewart Hall. Which wasn't nearly as bad as losing the woman he loved.

The thought that Cassie could be relatively happy with Edward by her side in the home she treasured was comforting to Julian.

"I do not know how I am to proceed, knowing that you are . . ." Cassie worked on strengthening her composure. "We must never be alone. Do you understand?"

Julian nodded, he knew exactly what she meant. Coming out here, being alone on the terrace with her was a mistake. The guests' conversation and the dancing music from the ballroom seemed to have resumed. The squire realized how foolish his action had been.

"I am to be married!" Her words were spoken in an emotional plea. "Please, you must promise me."

"As you say, this is difficult enough for us." Julian

gave a shallow bow of his head. "I give you my word."

"Until we meet again . . . in a more public venue." Cassie dipped a curtsy and left the terrace.

Julian watched Cassandra reenter the ballroom. He dare not follow directly. He did not want anyone to have the slightest notion that anything untoward had happened.

He watched her take Sir Horace's arm as he escorted her onto the dance floor. After a few moments, Julian thought it safe to proceed. Edward met him the instant he stepped inside.

"I say, Julian, had a go at one of the guests, did you? Aren't you the downy one?" Edward swiped his upper lip, indicating that his brother should mimic him. "For heaven's sake, Julian, wipe that lip paint off your mouth or everyone will know."

The squire drew a handkerchief from his coat pocket and removed the stain. The smudged rouge told him of his indiscretion.

"Glad to see you have it in you, old man." Edward slapped his brother's midsection with the back of his hand.

The squire eyed his brother. Edward would not have been so jolly about the news had he'd known it was Cassie who'd been kissed.

On his return to Stewart Hall, Julian once again isolated himself in the library. He peeled off his coat, tore the cravat from his neck and tossed them both aside.

He poured a glass of brandy, lifted the glass to his lips and froze, remembering that evening and those few precious moments he shared with Cassie.

He had promised her. He had given his word. He would not interfere. And by God, he was as good as his word.

He set the untouched glass on the table then sat at his desk. Closing his eyes for only a few seconds, he could clearly hear Cassie humming a song as they danced.

He jerked awake. Julian did not wish to fall asleep. He'd dream of *her*. He always did.

The squire donned his spectacles and pulled that day's correspondence toward him, determined to answer every missive upon his desk.

The sound of voices woke Julian and he raised his head off the desk.

He heard Cassie's voice.

Julian pushed himself up and moved to the door, pulling it open just an inch to peer through.

"Thank you for seeing me home safely. I am sorry to make you leave the ball so soon." Cassie stood with Edward at the end of the foyer.

"No matter, my dear. My bachelor days are numbered. This will give me a chance to stop by the clubs, play some cards. I shall not be staying out late once we're wed."

"I'm glad I did not ruin your evening, then."

"I never regret the chance to share your company." Edward led her to the staircase. "I wish you a good night, my dear."

Edward took Cassie into his arms for a kiss. Julian could not make himself watch the painful scene. He leaned back and closed the door.

Not more than a minute had passed before a small tap sounded from the door. Whoever it was did not wait for him to answer. The door ever so slowly opened and Lorna slipped through the narrow opening. Julian had never seen her look this miserable.

"Julian?" she whispered in a guilt-filled voice and moved toward the hearth where he sat in a leather chair.

"Shouldn't you be headed to bed?" The squire straightened, concern for his sibling overshadowing his personal problems. "What troubles you, poppet?"

"Tonight at the party," she whispered in the same soft hush. Her cheeks flushed with a deep, dark red.

"Did someone act improperly?" Julian's temper began to rise at the thought of some young buck making advances. He would see the fellow thrashed!

"I believe so," Lorna answered coolly.

"I demand you tell me who is responsible for the outrage!" He stood, readying himself to rush out of the house that very night and see justice done.

"*You,*" she said directly, her eyes accusing him.

Julian froze at the accusation.

"I saw you . . . on the terrace . . . you and Cassie."
The shock in her young voice and that she had wit-
nessed his duplicity. "You're in love with her, aren't
you?"

Julian's legs lost their strength and gave way,
dropping him back into the chair. How could he deny
it? "Yes . . . yes . . . I do love her." He closed his eyes
and clapped his hands over his face. Tears came to
his eyes.

"Does this mean she doesn't love Edward, she loves
you?" Lorna laid a comforting hand on his shoulder.
"Why don't you stop the wedding?"

"I can't . . . I gave her my word."

"But, you *love* her. Isn't that all that matters?" Lorna
looked upon her eldest brother.

"No, I'm afraid it doesn't. It's what we both have
to do," he confessed.

Julian could see it in her eyes. Lorna now realized
she no longer wished for a suitor like Edward as she
had always dreamed about. *He* was what she wanted
in a man. Someone who could love her deeply and
completely.

And maybe that's what the squire needed—
someone to care for him. If Cassie could find some
happiness without him, why couldn't he manage the
same?

Indeed, perhaps it was time he found a new wife. The night was still young . . .

Maxwell entered the room with a tray of coffee and set it on the table next to the desk. "I believe it is your wish to work throughout the night again, sir?"

"I was . . . but I have changed my mind." Julian pulled his discarded cravat from the floor and tried to shake the wrinkles from it.

"Have you, sir?"

"You know, Maxwell, I used to be like you." Julian straightened his collar and wound the linen around his neck.

"Were you, sir?"

"I used to have the same stern face." The squire patted Maxwell's cheek. "The same straightforward, stalwart stance." He patted Maxwell's chest in male camaraderie and imitated the butler's upright posture.

Maxwell's eyes continued to look forward and never once wavered.

"I just want to thank you for your efforts." Julian's head moved from side to side as he spoke.

"I'm sure I don't know to what you are referring, sir."

"You know very well to what I'm referring." Julian shook his finger at him. He moved near Maxwell's ear to whisper. "That little tryst you planned for Lady Cassandra and me." He backed away, his lips curled in an offish manner, his eyes seemed to move about. "Very clever plan."

"You credit me with more ingenuity than I am capable."

"I think not. I believe you were only looking out for my welfare." Julian tried to tie the neckcloth into some semblance of its previous knot. "But it was wrong, Maxwell. We should not have met." He pivoted toward the butler and pointed at his limp linen. "Do you think you could possibly . . ."

"I apologize, sir. I lack the proper skills for that type of delicate work. Perhaps I should send for Postlewait."

The squire groused and pushed the remaining lengths of linen into his vest. "That'll do."

"Perhaps if you had a good night's sleep, sir. Tomorrow evening might find you in better form, and I'm sure your valet would be delighted to sculpt your cravat into a spectacular—"

"I'm in fine form now, what?" The squire shrugged on the dark blue jacket he'd worn earlier at the ball.

"I am only voicing concern for your extended late night hours. I do not believe you have spent a single night in your bedchamber since—"

"Will you have the carriage brought around?" Julian brushed at the wrinkles he just noticed in his jacket sleeves. And he had the devil of a time trying to get them to disappear.

Maxwell headed for the door and turned back at

the last minute. "May I inquire if you will be return-ing to your study tonight?"

Julian raised his head regally and surveyed his sur-roundings. "I should say not. I"—the squire made a grand gesture high in the air with his arm—"shall be-come a man about town."

In the hours before daybreak, a light but insistent rapping came at Cassie's door. It woke her from a light and troubled slumber that had not come easy.

"What is it?" she asked from her sleepy state. The latch clicked open. Maxwell entered.

"Pardon the hour, my lady. An emergency has arisen. I believe the squire is seriously injured."

The news brought Cassie directly awake. Donning a robe and slippers she hurried out of her room after the butler.

"A disturbance at White's," he explained.

Two footmen carried a limp body up the stairs. Cassie rushed over, and Maxwell followed with the candelabrum. The footmen paused for an instant be-fore moving on.

"Julian!" she gasped and shot a stern look at Maxwell.

The momentum of the footmen carried them around the corner.

"I've instructed them to take him to his bedcham-ber. I'm afraid the library sofa, although it might be the squire's choice, would not be sufficient to accommodate him."

"Of course. You did the right thing, Maxwell."

"And I have taken the liberty and sent for the physician. I fear his injuries may be more serious than we can ascertain."

If she hadn't known better, Cassie might have thought a line of worry crossed the butler's usual unreadable face.

Cassie headed down the hall, following the footmen. The squire's body lay limp on a large four-poster bed.

Julian . . . what's happened?

He looked terrible. In the dim light, Cassie lifted his tousled hair from his forehead. Untying the bloodstained cravat, she gently removed it and unbuttoned his torn shirt which was soaked with blood—his blood. Pulling the sides open, she saw the darkened areas on his abdomen and she feared that he might have bruised or broken ribs.

She used clean linen and warm water Maxwell had brought to tend to Julian's superficial wounds. Wringing the water from the rag, Cassie began to clean the caked, dried blood from his face.

Bruises spotted his cheekbones, mostly on his left side. Setting the soiled cloth aside, she ran her cool hand along his injured face.

Alone in the room, she traced his lips with her fingers. She let them linger for just a moment before she noticed Maxwell's silent presence. She thought he had gone.

"The physician should arrive by daybreak . . . in about an hour, my lady."

"Did you wake Edward?" Cassie did not try to explain the intimate touch she knew Maxwell must have seen.

"Mr. Edward has not yet returned home."

"He's not back? He said he went out to play cards."

"Apparently they were not together," the butler calmly replied. "There are many clubs in London, my lady. It is quite possible he was at another."

Cassie glanced up at his response. If she had heard correctly, it was in a somewhat curious tone.

"If Mr. Edward were in the vicinity, he surely would have come to the squire's aid."

"Of course, you are right." She sighed, feeling foolish that she had read more into his answer. "Please send for Mrs. Green . . . then there will be two of us. I don't want the squire to be left alone." Cassie impatiently stood and glanced out the window. "Where is the physician?"

Chapter Fifteen

Dawn had broken with the physician's arrival. He stayed for nearly two hours tending to Julian. It had been almost three hours since he had left and Cassie still sat by the squire's bedside, unwilling to leave. Mrs. Green remained by her side for most of the early morning. She took a few minutes to run to the kitchen to bring something for Cassie to eat, despite her insistence she was not hungry.

Julian had not regained consciousness which was of great concern. The physician had no clue to why he was in this condition or how long it was to last.

In the dim glow of the candlelight, Cassie studied Julian's bedchamber. She could not see the entire room from where she sat in an upholstered armchair next to Julian, who lay on his solid four-poster bed.

The adorning bedcurtains were thick and heavy to keep out the daylight. Against the wall across from her she could make out a tall cabinet.

Heavy footsteps from the hallway grew louder. She doubted it was Maxwell. No one ever heard the butler enter or exit a room. Cassie straightened in her chair, wondering who the intruder might be.

The footfalls stopped abruptly and the visitor leaned into the room. "Julian? Julian, you in there?"

"Edward?"

"Cass? What the devil are you doing in there?" He hurried into the room. Edward did not look his usual, incomparable self. His hair was untidy, his clothing wrinkled. He smelled of spirits, cheroot smoke, and stale scent.

Is this what happened to men when they went out to play cards? They stayed out until the sun rose, came home smelling bad and looking worse? Surely he had been occupied with much more than ordinary gambling.

"I beg your pardon, my language." He looked from Cassie to Julian laid out on his bed, still. "Shouldn't there be a maid or footman watching over him?"

"He is badly hurt, Edward. The physician is very concerned that he has not awakened. Are you not worried?"

"Pfft, never . . . Julian is a robust individual."

"I cannot rest until I know he is well."

"Aren't you an angel." Edward neared, leaned

down, and kissed Cassie on top of her head. "You go ahead and play the ministering miss if it makes you feel better. I'm off to bed." He rubbed his face and shuffled to the door.

"Can you not make inquiries? Are you not at all concerned to what has happened to him? And who is responsible?"

"Julian can take care of himself. He always has." Edward jabbed his index finger at the motionless form on the bed and left.

An hour later, Julian moaned. Cassie rushed to his side, placing her hands gently upon him to keep him still. She hoped he wasn't in much pain.

He blinked open his eyes and smiled when he saw her. "Have I died? You're here. I think I'm in heaven."

"No, you are safe at Stewart Hall and the physician says you are in a bad state. You must rest."

"You shouldn't be here. You said we were not to be alone. Here you are in my bedchamber . . ." He made a move to sit upright, winced at the pain then thought better of it.

"Well, the circumstances have changed. I did not know you would be on death's door the very next day and . . . I was afraid for you." The confession seemed to ease the tension between them.

"Do not mistake me, I am glad you are here, if only to watch over me."

"Apparently, I am the only one who is. Well, Lorna will be when she learns of your condition, of course, but I am shocked over Edward's indifference. His family has always been of the utmost importance."

"It is not his place to worry about me. He is to marry you and his concern should be your new life together."

"If only there were a way we could manage . . ." At this moment Cassie's choice was clear if the decision of man or mansion had to be made. She sighed. "It does not signify. No matter what our outcome may be"—she pulled her hand free of his and stroked his face—"I shall always be here for you."

"And I," he said, placing his hand over hers. "Your devoted servant."

In two days, the mended squire ventured out of Stewart Hall into London. He would first stop at White's. Its front window was boarded and the inside was in a state of complete disrepair. George Raggett, the new owner, had been expecting Julian's full retribution for the damages incurred.

"Bought this place only a month ago, sir," Raggett explained. "I didn't expect the patrons in an establishment such as this to brawl as if in a common pub." He shook his head. "Who would have guessed that you started it all."

Julian said nothing but felt properly humbled.

He'd taken a swing at Lord Avery, who might have deserved to have his cork drawn, the squire couldn't remember. He hadn't been able to remember much from that night, only that he had, as Mr. Raggett stated, started a most undignified fight.

Sir Anthony Crenshaw was the kind soul who, with the assistance of a Mr. Hanford, had helped Julian leave the premises. It was also Sir Anthony who had seen the squire to his transport and sent him home.

"It's not just the window . . . I'll be closed until they finish repairs."

The squire glanced over at the rubble: The broken furniture, glasses, lamps, chairs, and most particularly the large front window through which he had made his undignified exit.

Of course he was responsible. He was also anxious to be on his way. It was his last stop that weighed heavy upon his mind. He pulled out a bank draft and offered it to the owner.

"That should more than compensate you for your trouble, I should think."

Raggett glanced at the figure and his eyes grew large. "Oh, yes. Thank you, sir. Thank you, very much." He now gazed at the devastation with appreciation. "I had thought to make a change. Put the door where the window is and perhaps something to distinguish the place, a bow window, there." He pointed at the existing doorway.

"Good man, have at it." Without offering a word of apology, Julian clapped the owner on the back and left.

Still sporting the cuts and bruises of the brawl, Julian did not need to touch his tender, blackened eye to remind him of the pain. Nothing could come close to the ache of his broken heart.

Yet he wondered if there was a chance that he and Cassandra . . . no, he loved her too much to ask her to sacrifice the home she held so dear and completely disregard their fathers' wishes. They could not—*he* could not do such a thing.

Julian had to ignore his feelings. But what if Cassandra was to insist? He would have to deal with that when and if it happened. The squire could not waste time pondering wishful thoughts and had to get back to the business at hand. Next he was to secure a special license for the upcoming wedding.

He pulled himself up into the carriage. It felt as if his side tore open with the movement. Once seated he rapped on the trapdoor.

"Where to, squire?" the driver asked.

"To the office of the archbishop."

With the increasing influx of people, florists, tailors, and caterers and a multitude of others over the course of the week, the finality of Cassandra's marriage loomed over the squire. Madam Bosqué came out to do the bridal fitting personally which further reminded him of the importance of the upcoming event.

From the open door of the library, Julian saw the

French modiste and her assistants usher the boxes that comprised the pieces of the bride's wedding wardrobe into the house and up the staircase. He wished he could feel the excitement upon seeing the woman he loved, wearing the bridal gown, instead of the dread that came upon him at every one of the dressmaker's visits.

He closed the door after the day's procession had left and again ignored the summons for dinner. He remained in the library, bent over documents and papers, scratching out portions of letters only to rewrite them several more times without making their meanings clear. He finally told himself that he could not continue to hide. In two days the wedding would be upon them.

The next morning, Julian set his coffee cup on the breakfast table and eased into the chair intent on reading his morning paper.

The bumps and bruises on his face and arms were nearly healed. His ribs were another matter—the pain on his side continued to plague him, a constant reminder of his foolish behavior at the club.

Romeo came trotting in and right up to the squire. "Nice to see you, old thing," Julian greeted him.

Romeo whined then lifted his front end into an upright sitting position, begging. When the squire did not show any sign of rewarding this display of talent, the canine proceeded to exhibit his entire repertoire.

He ran in a circle to the left then to the right, stood

on his hind legs, and rolled over, landing once again on his feet.

"I applaud you. It's all very well done." Julian chuckled which made his sides ache. "Come now, you know your mistress forbids us to hand you scraps from the table." He scolded Romeo. "However, I shall keep a dish to give to you later. I'm sure she will not object."

Women's voices rang outside in the corridor. When Cassandra and Lorna appeared in the doorway, Julian stood. He and Cassandra locked gazes and he nearly forgot his sister was also in the room until she spoke.

"I shall be just a moment, Lady Cassandra. I need to inform Mrs. Upton that we've returned." Lorna backed out of the room then called for Romeo once she reached the hall.

A precious silence followed and for the next minute neither spoke. Julian was merely glad to share her company, a distinct pleasure of having her all to himself.

"Good morning, my lady," he said and the warm affection his words held was evident even to him.

"Good day to you, sir." Her voice was soft and understated.

Moments later Edward entered. "I happen to have heard that exchange," came the accusation, and a wide smile upon his face. "Look at what progress you've made since my absence." He stepped between them and held out his arms. "I can feel great affection here." He gestured from Cassie to Julian and back. "I truly believed if you both made an effort you could rub along famously. This could not make me happier. You are looking in fine form today, brother."

"I am doing tolerably well, considering," the squire replied and winced.

"What did I tell you, my lady? Julian has fared well, there was no reason to worry." With a tilt of his head, Edward addressed Julian. "Did you know that she had refused to leave your bedside? Only when—"

Maxwell's presence at the doorway silenced him. "Misters Whitmore and Sutherland have arrived for you, sir."

"I shall be there presently." Edward nodded to the butler. "This is my last bit of work before I leave on my wedding trip. You'd best break out your traveling cloak, brother, and prepare to take my place while I'm gone." He turned to Cassandra. "I'm off, my dear. The next time I see you might be at the altar tomorrow." Edward smiled, obviously looking forward to their impending nuptials. He bowed over her hand. "I wish the two of you a most delightful day."

Cassie moved to the sideboard and poured herself a cup of coffee. Julian remained standing until she took her seat.

"I never did thank you for watching over me." He folded his morning paper and placed it to one side.

"I was only there for a short time. But I was quite worried that night. The next day, the physician concluded that your injury wasn't as bad as he had originally feared. Maxwell told him that it had been ages since you'd been properly to bed. The entire time you were unconscious it seems that you were merely catching up on your sleep." Cassie chanced a look at him. "You must have been exhausted."

"I must admit that I have had a difficult time of late. I'm sure after the wedding has passed the house will return to its normal routine."

Although his words came easily, she did not imagine that it would be simple for him to return to his life, as it had been, before her.

Cassie wondered if he had second thoughts, as she had. That following their fathers' dreams would turn out nightmarish wrong for everyone.

Again she thought of that night in his bedchamber. How she would willingly give up her home to spend the rest of her life with him. But the scandal it would bring upon their families . . . they might never regain any kind of respectability.

Lorna, followed by Romeo, entered the breakfast room and came to a stop. "Am I interrupting?" She stared at them wide-eyed.

"No, please stay, Lorna," they said simultaneously.

"Very well." She looked from one to the other. "I

suppose I shall. It seems the two of you so adamantly wish it."

It was true. Lorna's presence as chaperone, the both of them knew, would be the only way they could be trusted not to misbehave.

It was the morning of her wedding. Cassie stared at her reflection in the full-length glass. She wore a simple high-waisted white silk gown with satin stitch embellishments. A strand of pearls twisted through her artfully styled hair. She would not describe the bride she saw as radiant. That implied she glowed with happiness and anticipation of her married life.

Married. The word echoed in her mind.

She knew that she was about to make the biggest mistake of her life. She hadn't thought so yesterday but she was beginning to think so now.

A knock sounded at her door. She was terrified it might be Edward with another thoughtful gift or even worse, it might be Julian. Cassie had no idea how she could face him now.

The door eased open and Lorna poked her head into the room.

"Lorna, do come in." A wonderful feeling of relief swept through Cassie on seeing a friendly face.

Lorna entered with Romeo at her heels. "How very beautiful you look." The compliment did not match the unhappiness in her eyes. "Romeo and I picked these wildflowers for you to carry."

"How very kind. Thank you."

"I thought if we tied a ribbon around the stems . . ." Then she stopped and her eyes filled with tears. "I saw you at Lady Cowper's party. You and Julian—kissing."

Cassie remembered how unexpected and wonderful that kiss was. Her greatest fear had been they would be seen and now . . . as it turned out, they had been.

"Belinda did not see, of course. I distracted her," she told Cassie. "But I saw you. I spoke to Julian about it, that very night. He loves you, I know he does, and he won't do anything about it. He won't stop the wedding. I don't understand why he won't—"

"He *can't*." Cassie did not want to listen to how much he loved her or how much he cared for her. "He promised me he would not interfere. I must marry Edward."

"But why? Julian loves you, I know he does. And I can tell you love him too."

"How shall I explain?" Cassie sat on her bed and motioned for Lorna to sit next to her. "If I do not marry Edward, I will lose my home—Hedgeway Park. If I were to break the engagement with Edward and marry Julian, it would be a horrible scandal, our family would be ruined. We must consider your future, your prospects for a match."

"Jeffrey will marry me. He doesn't care, he loves me!" Lorna stared at her folded hands in her lap. Her sorrow was genuine and heartfelt. She met Cassie's gaze. "Is there no way you can have both your home and the husband you desire?"

"Not any way I can foresee."

The furniture in the large parlor had been pushed aside, making way for enough chairs to accommodate the small gathering of guests. It surprised Cassie that she knew everyone in attendance. Lorna and her friend Belinda, their beaux Jeffrey Rutherford and Thomas Wentworth stood near the large-paned window. The trio of Corinthians—Daniel Thompson, Jared Gilbert, and Colin Henderson—all friends of Edward's, gathered a few steps behind him. Also attending was Sir Horace Boyer, friend of the squire, and finally Julian himself. Dressed in a coat of dark blue, buff breeches, and top boots, he looked dashing enough to be the groom.

Edward approached her and held out his arm. "You are a beauty beyond compare."

Cassie took his arm and thanked him. He led her through the guests toward the priest who stood with bible in hand.

"We are gathered here in the sight of God . . ."

What was she going to do? Stand here and wed Edward against her will . . . it wasn't what Cassie wanted. The scandal that she thought would touch their families now seemed unimportant. Hedgeway

Park, although it was her beloved home, was only a pile of stone compared to the companionship and affection of the man she loved. And she hadn't realized until this moment that he was truly the one she could not live without.

Was it too late to stop this madness? She looked over to the smiling Edward, handsome in his exquisitely cut, dark grey jacket and Hessians. He would not be so happy if he knew of her misery. The squire, who stood next to the groom, somber and drawn, would never interfere. She had made him promise. Cassie had to end this, and now was the precise, appropriate moment . . .

"If anyone here knows of just cause that this marriage should not take place, speak now or forever hold your peace," the priest said then paused.

The voice within Julian Stewart shouted at him to speak now. This was his last chance to stop this farce before it was final. Cassandra was the only woman he had ever loved. He was certain that remaining silent would result in a lifetime of regret for both of them.

Julian's throat went dry as he willed himself to act. He swallowed hard and mustered all of his courage. He opened his mouth to voice his objection. He willed himself to step forward, hold his hand high in the air and shout—

"Stop at once!" A heavily French-accented baritone cried out, filling the room. The bride and groom dropped hands and turned to face the gentleman.

Julian hadn't a chance to raise his hand or to speak, he looked toward the doorway. A well-dressed elderly man made his way to the altar where Cassandra and Edward stood.

Then the squire detected the slightest whiff of jasmine.

Chapter Sixteen

"**I** most completely object to zis marriage!" The man advanced to the front of the gathering.

"May I ask what the objection is?" the priest inquired, closing his book.

"You . . . we thought zat you were dead!" He stared at Edward as if he was regarding an apparition. "It eez of a most private matter. I will speak to za squire, if you please. I am Monsieur Dubois."

"Monsieur Dubois," Julian said.

"You do not know me?" He squinted from the elder brother to the younger as if he was suspicious.

"I am afraid not, should I?" Julian also looked to Edward for an answer.

"Young man"—Dubois addressed Edward with controlled rage—"what do you think you are doing 'ere?"

"I believe we should adjourn to a more private setting until we can straighten this out," Julian said softly to the people around him. He raised his voice for guests to hear, "Your attention, everyone! There is a matter we need to clear before we proceed. I apologize for the delay."

The crowd began to talk among themselves and the murmur grew. Maxwell stood at the doorway.

"If everyone would please be patient, we shall resume as soon as possible," Julian told them.

"Honored guests, if you all would be so kind as to follow me." The butler led the small group, including the priest, out of the front parlor.

After the wedding guests left, Julian led the wedding party to the library. Cassandra, the squire noticed, followed but lagged behind.

Waiting inside, a lovely, and very pregnant chestnut-brown–haired young lady sat in a chair, her jasmine perfume filling the library. Julian could just imagine exactly what Dubois' objection was.

Edward strode to the young lady's side and whispered something.

" 'Ow dare you!" she shrieked. "Do not *mon cherie* me. I thought you were dead! I *wish* you were!"

"As you see, I am well, Marie." Edward chuckled. "No harm has befallen me." He was clearly trying to keep her calm.

"*Cochon!*" She made to strike him but he stepped aside, missing the blow.

"I was merely seeing to her comfort," he said in his own defense to Julian.

"We came to zee about the circumstances concerning *his* death"—Dubois pointed at Edward— "And what do we find? You are marrying yet another woman!"

Marie broke out into an uncontrollable, and very loud, bout of tears.

"He eez already married to my daughter. Marie has bore him two children, another eez on zee way!"

Marie and Cassandra looked at the other. They redirected their piercing gazes at Edward who appeared to be relatively unconcerned at the women's mutual revulsion of him.

"It would seem that you are the only one who knows the various parties involved, Edward. Would you be so kind as to do the necessary?"

Julian allowed his brother to step forward. Everyone remained momentarily quiet and relatively calm as the introductions and explanations were made.

"I was only doing what was expected of me," Edward offered. It was a poor excuse. "Well, Marie was in France and Cass, you are—"

"How dare you make me a part of bigamy!" Cassandra slapped Edward's face with her right hand.

Julian flinched. He knew what it was like being on the receiving end of that.

With tears streaming down her face, she ran from the room. Torn between the need to comfort her or to remain and sort out this terrible muddle, Julian decided to stay.

"Edward, I will deal with you later." The squire turned away from his brother. "Mademoiselle, Monsieur Dubois—"

"It eez Madame Stewart," she corrected him with her chin held high, unashamed of her bulging belly.

"Ah yes, I beg your pardon." Julian bowed his head respectfully. "You and your father are welcome to stay at Stewart Hall."

"Merci, sir, after witnessing zis disgrace, my daughter and I plan to return 'ome as soon as possible." Marie wept and leaned heavily on her father's arm. "With or without 'er 'usband!"

"I understand, monsieur," Julian said. "Maxwell can attend to the details and show you to your rooms where you may remain for as long as you need."

The butler stood in the doorway and led them away, leaving the two brothers.

"How could you treat her like that? She is your wife," Julian scolded once he knew they could not be overheard. "That girl is in love with you."

"So is Cass." A confident smile crossed Edward's face. He flopped into one of the chairs, at complete ease and unfettered by the current circumstance.

Julian shook his head. "There you're wrong." His brother was not going to win this time. "Cassandra doesn't love you. She's in love with me." Saying it out loud was such a wonderful feeling.

"You? Don't be daft!" Edward did not for a minute believe it was true. "When she could have me?"

"In outside of an hour the whole of London will know you're married—and not to Lady Cassandra." Julian hadn't meant his words to sound like a threat. "Your reputation with your *many* lady friends will be ruined."

The expression on Edward's face grimmed. He shifted in the chair, recrossing his legs. That thought must not have occurred to him. "You're enjoying all this aren't you, Julian?"

"No. I'm disappointed in you. You've let our family down, not to mention the scandal that may ensue."

"Let you down? How can you say that? After I was caught in a compromising position I didn't abandon Marie, I married her. I've sent her money, kept her in comfort. She's been living with her friends and family, happy. She's ruined everything by coming here." Edward poked an accusing finger at his brother. "It was you and father who wanted me to marry Cass. I was more than willing to go through with it—without consideration to my own wishes."

"What were you giving up? You still parade around like a young buck, eligible to all the ladies in the ton. You carry on with no regard to the consequence or how it will affect those around you."

"Why shouldn't I? I'm happy. They're happy. Isn't that all that matters?"

"I'm afraid you don't see the seriousness of the matter. Marriage is a responsibility between two people, a commitment for life."

Edward shook his head. "If you think Cass will have you now, you're sadly mistaken."

"Why?"

"If she can't marry me, she'll lose her precious home. And you'll be the one taking it away from her." A disgusting grin spread over his face. "What do you think she'll feel for you then?"

Julian stood silent. "You are no longer welcome at Stewart Hall." He wouldn't let Edward have the satisfaction of seeing him show any kind of weakness. "I expect you to be packed up and out of this house immediately. If you're smart, you'll accompany your wife home to France." He walked to his desk.

Edward raked his brother with a scathing look and stalked out without a farewell.

As soon as Julian's anger subsided, the meaning of his brother's words struck him. Without marriage to Edward, Cassandra would lose her home.

Tomorrow, Julian would have to inform her that since she had not complied to her father's wishes, the ownership of Hedgeway Park would pass on to the present Earl of Thaddbury.

How would Julian ever face her after that pronouncement? Could she forgive him for being the instigator of her worst possible fear?

"You, sir, are the source of the problem." He addressed the will as if he spoke to the late earl himself.

The squire flung the wretched document across the room, disappointed it missed the hearth and did not catch fire.

What am I to do now?

Drawing the special license from his pocket, he wondered if he had any chance with Cassandra or was that merely wishful thinking on his part.

The squire barely noticed Maxwell enter. The butler lifted the document from the floor. Smoothing the rumpled pages one by one, in silence, he returned it to the desk and placed it in front of the squire.

Julian regarded Maxwell and had to take a second look. "Maxwell, is that a smile on your face?"

The butler's normal visage of indifference returned. Julian had never seen Maxwell show expression of any kind.

"What is it?" It wasn't in the butler's character to stare or gawk.

"I believe this document was drafted years after you, yourself, had a similar agreement with your late wife and her family."

"Yes, father had arranged marriages for both Edward and I when we were mere children." Julian knew the butler had understood the circumstances—he had worked for the previous squire. "We both understood what was expected of us when we reached our maturity."

"I do not presume to know the language of legalese and I would never intentionally pry into your personal matters, sir. However, as I retrieved the document, I could not help but notice a paragraph that I believe might have referenced Lady Cassandra's marriage before her twentieth birthday."

"The one naming Edward as her future groom. Yes, yes." Julian stood up from his chair, impatient. He'd read it more than a dozen times these past few days.

"I may be mistaken, but I do not recall, precisely, seeing his name, in particular, mentioned."

"What? What are you talking about?" Julian took the document and scanned each page until he found the clause to which Maxwell referred. "'Pon my word." His face brightened with a renewed sense of hope. "This . . . what it says here . . . it says . . . this says the son of Henry Stewart."

"It would appear so."

"We thought—we always *knew* it was Edward who was to marry her." The document astounded Julian— who thought he had read every word with the utmost care.

"You had been in the early years of your marriage yourself when your father departed. I'm sure you gave no additional thought to *who* would wed Lady Cassandra when the earl passed." Maxwell paused. "However the circumstances of your family have changed. Mr. Edward has a wife, while you are the available sibling."

"Which means . . . *I* could marry her." Julian couldn't believe it. This was incredible. How had he ever overlooked this? "I could marry her and she would meet the terms for her inheritance."

"I believe you are correct, sir." A small smile graced Maxwell's face.

Julian scrambled for the special license, forgetting where he had set it only moments before.

"Could this be what you are searching for?" Maxwell held out the folded parchment.

How did he get a hold of it? Maxwell hadn't gone near the desk. Julian decided now was not the time to delve into Maxwell's mysteries.

"Send for the vicar at once!"

"Vicar, sir?" Maxwell cleared his throat. "I believe that the priest has not yet left the house. He is presently in the dining room partaking of Madeira and fresh strawberry tarts with the rest of the guests." Maxwell clasped his hands behind his back.

"Get him! Get them all!" Julian blew around the room, excited and uncertain to what he should do first. "Tell them we're still going to have a wedding!"

Cassie left the library and ran to her room. Lavette chased after her, chattering in French, and Romeo ran alongside them, barking above their din.

"But 'oo is she? Where did she come from?" The maid followed Cassie all the way into her bed-chamber.

"I don't know, Lavette. I didn't ask."

"But she eez the wife of Monsieur Edward, eez she not?"

"Please, leave me!" Cassie desperately wanted to be left alone. She chased the maid out the door and closed it behind her. Cassie felt so ashamed, humiliated.

Without a knock, the bedchamber door opened. Cassie did not have time to prevent her visitor's entry. She turned and faced the door in time to see that it was *him.*

"Julian, please." Cassie wiped at her tear-stained face. Perhaps she could speak to him tomorrow or the day after when she had calmed. "I don't think I can—"

He moved close to her, trying to gather her in his arms, but she would not allow him near.

"I have ordered Edward away from the house," he told her. "I tried to encourage him to remain with his wife. It seemed to me that she wasn't the *understanding* type or perhaps it is her delicate condition that's made her disagreeable. In any case, I'll bet he'll have a rough go of it."

And hearing that, somehow, made Cassie feel a little better.

"It will be a very long time until he is welcomed back to Stewart Hall."

"Is that it, then?" Now that Edward was gone, or would be shortly, there was no need for a wedding. She glanced at Julian. Yes, she loved him and she was certain he still loved her.

And perhaps they would marry. When that day came, they would cause a further disgrace upon their families by marrying so soon after the initial scandal. It was comforting to know that it would most certainly be a very long time until she had to face that day.

"I had thought to stop the ceremony moments before Monsieur Dubois arrived," the squire confessed.

"So did I," Cassie admitted.

Julian held her by both arms and stared into her eyes. "If you marry me today, right now, you will remain the owner of Hedgeway Park."

"What? How is that possible?"

"It is in accordance to your father's will—something I overlooked."

"But how are we to manage on such short notice?" Cassie could not believe that it was possible.

"By special license." He smiled and pulled the parchment from his jacket pocket.

"But how is it you happen to have . . ." How had he acquired one? When had that been?

"You should have seen the look on the clerk's face when I applied for two licenses and named the same bride on each. I told him the lady was fickle."

"Fickle?" Cassie raised her hand to slap his face. Julian caught her wrist before she could strike.

"You see, you don't even know if you want to kiss me or slap me." He chuckled in good humor.

"I think I wish to slap you," she said with a playful certainty.

"I think not." He drew her toward him and enveloped her in his arms. "I am quite certain you want to kiss me."

She met his lips with hers. Nothing ever felt so perfect, so right. It was difficult to comprehend this was actually happening.

"You are dressed to be wed and the guests are below, waiting to attend the ceremony. What do you say, Lady Cassandra? Will you marry me?" The softness of his voice bespoke a tenderness she had not felt from him previously.

Yes, of course, I want to marry you.

It was the best Cassie could ever have wished for, the man she loved proposing a match she desired.

"I do not ask for your hand to save your precious Hedgeway Park nor do I ask out of duty because our fathers wished to unite our families. I ask you to become my wife because I love you." He kissed her hand and waited for her answer.

"I accept." It was all she could do to contain her joy. Cassie gladly told him, "I, too, love you, sir."

"Let us be wed. Then off to our new home Hedgeway Park." He took her hand and placed it in the crook of his arm before quitting the room. "Where, I am quite certain, we shall live happily ever after."